THROWING STONES

THROWING STONES

for Jean,
here's to throwing stones
+ making ripples!
love
Gwenyth

Gwenyth Perry

Bookcaster Press Limited

First published in New Zealand December 1998
by Bookcaster Press Limited
PO Box 3765
Auckland

Printed and bound in Auckland, New Zealand.

The cover painting by Sydney Lough Thompson
is reproduced with the kind permission of
Madame Yseult Annette Thompson in France.

A Bookcaster Press book.
ISBN 0-473-05654-2

To the memory of you,

still smiling in the mind's eye.

THROWING STONES

You throw a stone
into the silent pond.
Ripples shatter
our double reflection
as the words just spoken
break our duality
into waves
circling
in opposite directions.

You have thrown
too many stones.
The glass of our lives
proves too fragile.

Chapter One

Oddly enough she suddenly remembers the number of times she was asked, as a child: "What are you going to be when you grow up?"

"A fairy queen," she would reply, pirouetting in front of the patronising smiling adults. Later she would recognise the patronage and become more evasive.

"Prime Minister," she would say defiantly, or "Judge," knowing that their indulgent smiles ruled her out of contention because she was only a girl. She had learnt by then that adults did not take her seriously, that they hardly heard her replies before turning away to talk about something else, concentrating on each other.

It puzzled her that the situation did not seem to change as she got older. No-one took her seriously. She was just a dizzy girl with her head in a book and nothing of significance to say in the real world. Nobody wanted to know what she thought, what she felt, what she really wanted to do. She seemed to live on the edge of the world trying to make a dent in it. Even if she did, Paula felt that no-one would notice.

So how did she get from there to here? A suburban kitchen. Well it is only a small provincial town, not really big enough to have suburbs. She, Paula the dreamer, is standing at her kitchen sink gazing out the window into the trees at the bottom of their well tended garden, dreaming. Still dreaming, and remembering.

What happened to that early dreamer? Why did she allow herself to be seduced by someone else's dreams? Her life was taken over by Gordon, and she let it happen, indeed willed it to happen, once she fell for his clean profile, his seductive tongue, his own ambitions, which she has to admit seemed much more realistic and practical than her own.

So here she is. Two neat, clean, quite averagely well behaved children, a boy and a girl of course, both safely away at school, while she tidies an immaculate kitchen and prepares to leave for her part time work in the town's only bookshop.

It's only now that she's beginning to think of those other dreams. She looks at the letter again. The letter that stirs up all those old memories and hopes, making her feel restless and dissatisfied with herself, her life. The letter from Eleanor on the other side of the world. The written words make both the years and the distance fall away as she reads. This missile from the past, shot off to shatter her peace.

Dear Paula,
Yes well. I know I'm a lousy letter writer, and don't remind me that it's been ten years. I knew you wouldn't have moved. Hec, Gordon was set in rock in that town. Own business, own place in it. I never could understand why you went along, but you seemed happy. I hope you still are. Those kids you were gooing over with such disgusting indulgent delight must be real monsters by now. Hope you still manage to enjoy them. Not me. No kids. Couldn't have stuck with one man either. How have you?
Yes I'm alone again. Don't need a Gordon though so don't you think it. Never did. Never will.
Just felt like trying to communicate with the friend I used to know. To see if she's still there somewhere, not totally buried in small town domesticity. Hell Polly you never even travelled. Haven't you ever wanted to break out, find some wider horizons? Believe me they're wide. I could never come back now.
What I'm really meaning to say is, those kids of yours must be old enough by now. Good old

Gordon and mother down the road could surely manage without you for a while. She'll still be alive. Her sort never die. How could you live in the same town all these years?

Suppose I'm making assumptions. Always did probably. You could be long gone, divorced, career womaned, remarried. Somehow I think not. You'll still be there.

You deserve some time off woman. Take it. Come and join me. You must be pretty rich by now with good old Gordon. What do you spend it on? Did you ever get to travel with him? Bet he wouldn't. So you do it. Come. For as long as you like. I've got this small place in France for the summer. A friend's loaned it to me. In Brittany, near the coast. Remember how we used to dream of going to France together? Haven't you ever envied me for doing it? You'd love it, Polly. Time you did it yourself. For yourself. Have you ever done anything for yourself, not just Gordon and the kids?

I'll shut up now in case I overstate my case, as those lecturers always used to tell me I did. Think about it, pal. You've got a couple of months. I'm at this address till some time in April, then Poste Restante, Concarneau. Doesn't that grab you? Come.

Love,

YoP,

Eleanor.

Paula takes the washing out of the machine and lugs it out to the line. It hangs limply, no wind at all. The neat rows of Gordon's cabbages and beans gaze up at her. Not a daring white butterfly in sight. Grapes hang heavily on the back fence, passion-fruit in one corner, kiwifruit, a neatly mated pair, in the other. It's no longer what she wants to see.

Eleanor's words haunt her, echo in her brain. Apart

3

from anything else, it seems a lifetime since anyone called her Polly, or signed off with the old pal signal.

Has she ever done anything for herself? She thinks back to the last time she saw Eleanor, twelve years before. Then two years of spasmodic cards from different places before the long silence.

Eleanor came down to see her, stayed several nights. They talked late, reminiscing about their past as students, the only thing they had in common any more. The two small children interrupted their days, with only a brief respite when she left Simon at the playgroup and managed to get Emma to have a sleep at the same time.

Paula noticed the expression in her friend's eyes. The incomprehension of how anyone could cope with such demands on a daily basis. Eleanor looked glamorous, from another world. Stylishly dressed, her blonde hair sleek and well cut, her nails manicured, her smart little car glistening red in the driveway.

Eleanor stayed on at university when Paula left, her degree completed and Gordon's ring on her finger. Eleanor sailed through a second degree, taking honours in law, then a job with an international company creating New Zealand links in Auckland. She did well, earned well, was easily able to set her sights on overseas work, was already travelling with the company. This time she had come to say goodbye because she was finally leaving for good. They wanted to send her to Zurich. They both knew it was only a start, that she might not even stay with that company. It was the first time she visited without a striking male partner in tow. The latest one was already in Europe. She may or may not join him.

That time Paula saw her as someone from an alien world, completely outside her own understanding, her own reality. It did not occur to her to want the same things, to even consider them possible for herself. She adored her Gordon, doted on the children, wanted nothing else. Eleanor gone was Eleanor forgotten, those bright cards an occasional flash of light that made her smile, without envy.

This time the communication makes her think. Even makes her wonder how much she does still adore Gordon, dote on the children. Simon has already been away at boarding school for two years, the local high school not good enough for Gordon's children. His first major exam is this year. Emma has just started her boarding school. The long term stretches ahead quite empty with only herself and Gordon at home. She still hopes to expand her part time work, but she knows Miss Gray will be reluctant to relinquish any more control. It might come though. It was a major concession to let her go to the Booksellers' Conference when Miss Gray was unwell.

It has not occurred to Paula to look beyond the bookshop, even beyond the town. What will Gordon say?

She is beginning to realise she cares less and less what he says. She cannot stop herself from thinking how wonderful it would be to finally use some of the French from her degree, however rusty it might have become. Sure, Eleanor was the linguist, sailing through both French and German in that first degree, even Latin, while Paula tagged along with only French, concentrating more on history and English literature. She remembers the pleasure of discovering she could read French writers in the original, the one thing she has kept on doing whenever she has a chance to get hold of French novels.

Then there's history. In Europe. Her heart gives a lurch. What indeed has happened to all those dreams and plans she and Eleanor used to talk about? Can it really be time to do something she wants to do for herself?

Paula is pensive as she puts the laundry basket away and gets her bag ready for work. As she drives into town her mind goes back nearly two decades to an Auckland park. Among other first year students she and Eleanor lie on the grass, between lectures. She can hear their voices again, still fresh in her mind.

"I'm glad my name's different, special. Not just another Mary or Susan."

"Eleanor. Yes. It sounds romantic, medieval. Straight out of poetry."

"Yours is good too."

"Not really. Pauline might have been. Paula sounds as if my parents really wanted a boy. They did, of course."

"But then they got one. Stephen."

Paula looked at her friend, surrounded by daisies in the green grass, shaded by huge English trees away from the formal flower-beds.

"I haven't thought much about my name. I'd rather be incognito, just melt into the world."

"Why? Is that what you want?"

"Could have its advantages."

"I'd rather be distinctive. Make everyone remember me."

"You will. You'll be an actress, a famous writer, at least."

"But so will you."

"Oh no. I don't want to be looked at."

Paula's straight brown hair fell over her face, the too large brown eyes waif like in the narrow features as she regarded her generously endowed friend. Abundant blonde hair, prodigal mouth, noble blue eyes. Yes. The world would want to look at Eleanor. Paula pushed back a lank strand of her own hair with her thin brown arm.

"I'd rather make an impact. Change things."

"What?"

"You know. Do something lasting about hunger, unemployment, world problems."

"Crusader!" Eleanor said it almost as a dirty word. "I'd rather enjoy life."

"You will, you will. Probably I will too, but not the next hour if we're late for another tutorial."

They gathered their books and headed across to the old grey stone, surrounded by newer aluminium and glass.

Yes, Paula did have dreams. Even dreams of fame and glory, of making people look at her. Not just at Eleanor for her beauty and intelligence, but at her, Paula, for her real achievements. She dreamed of no longer being on the fringes looking in, but in the middle, controlling, looking out at the world. A world that would listen to what she had to say.

And here she is, still feeling as if she never has had anything to say.

Chapter Two

"Some more books have come from Penguin. There's the box. Could you mark off the docket and then put them out please?"

Miss Gray is already sorting through accounts and the shop is empty when Paula arrives. They have an hour together before Miss Gray takes time off for lunch, to do the banking, then to go home and feed her cats. Paula likes having the shop to herself. Wednesday is Roz's free afternoon, so at one o'clock they usually meet for lunch in the coffee bar along the road. If they feel stressed or daring they go to the pub, to have a glass of wine with a substantially loaded plate of chips and salad with steak, fish, or occasionally chicken. There is no other choice, as the other pubs do not go in for real pub food, or indeed any sort of dining room.

"Ready?" Roz arrives soon after Miss Gray's return. Paula prefers her not to be there before Miss Gray. Roz doesn't have far to come from the kindergarten where she works, but usually she has plenty to do before leaving. "Where'll we go?"

"I think I need a drink today. Let's go to the Strand."

"Sure." Miss Gray nods that she can leave. Roz looks at her quizzically as they walk along the lazy main street.

"What's brought this on?"

Paula waits until they're seated in one of the huge old wooden booths at the side of the dark panelled house bar, well away from the noise and bustle in the public bar. She knows how well her friend can read her, she will have to make some explanation, although she should probably tell Gordon first. She's bursting to tell someone.

8

"I've had a letter. From an old student friend I haven't heard from for about ten years."

"Goodness. Where is she, or he? Why the stunned look on your face?"

"She's in London. But she wants me to go and stay with her, in France."

"Lucky you! What a marvellous invitation!"

"It's not as easy as that."

"'Course it is."

"Yes, but..."

"No buts! I'd be jumping up and down. Aren't you excited?"

"Yes, but I haven't told anyone yet..."

"I'd be shouting it from the rooftops. Too much time working with books is shrivelling you up."

"I haven't had time to get used to the idea."

"Hey, your glass is empty. Let's get a whole bottle to celebrate."

"No! I have to work!"

Paula protests but there's no stopping Roz. The first glass certainly vanished. Maybe she'll have a stodgy dessert today as well, to soak it up.

"Let's plan how you're going to approach Gordon. He owes you a trip, he's hardly ever home."

"Well, it's only during the week when he has to travel round."

"You've done a marvellous job defending him all these years. Take a break yourself."

"I'd be scared to travel alone."

"Rubbish. Your friend will be at the other end."

Paula looks across at Roz, whose red hair is brushed back from her open freckled features. She's heartily tucking in to her steak and chips. Paula toys with her own fish, inconsequentially thinking of the meal she will cook for Gordon tonight, wondering if he will be late back for it from the branch thirty kilometres away. The wine seems to be going quite quickly. As Roz fills both glasses again, Paula heaps her fork with chips.

"Heh, you're in one of the new plays. My one! Will

you still be here?"

Paula laughs. They've both been involved with the local repertory group for so long it hasn't even come into her thoughts.

"I should think so, won't I?" She cannot imagine life beyond that point. It's impossible to think that she could actually fly away, on her own.

"I love Chekhov. It's great that we're doing all those super short plays." Roz is launched and Paula lets the conversation flow on. It's a baked pudding day, so they draw out the meal with huge helpings followed by coffee. It's pleasant to fill her lunch hour eating and talking. It seems a bit unfair to take a whole hour when she only starts work at eleven, but Miss Gray urged her to do so right from the beginning.

She's almost late. There's an unusual rush of customers, so she has no time to think for a while. Finally they have a break, with the mid afternoon cup of tea, made in the tiny back store room. Paula sighs with relief as she sits down, shaking herself a little to dispel the sleepiness brought on by the wine.

"You're looking a bit tired. Not sickening for anything, are you?" Miss Gray looks at her shrewdly through the old fashioned glasses.

"Oh no. Probably ate too much at lunch. We went to the hotel." She resists the temptation to spill her news again, and Miss Gray pours more tea.

Soon they're busy with the drift of children on their way home from school. Miss Gray does not like children very much. It's Paula's job to stand guard on the magazine and comic section to make sure they do not linger too long reading. She never stops them though unless Miss Gray looks over at one who's settled down for a good session. The children have her sympathy, and she knows that the regulars will be back to spend their pocket money on what they can afford.

When the rush is over, Paula goes to clear the mail box. In the bundle is one of Miss Gray's occasional letters with a London postmark. Miss Gray just opens the accounts and puts the airmail envelope in her bag to take home. She once said it was an old friend with a bookshop in London. She sometimes receives parcels of books with the same postmark.

Paula looks at her boss speculatively, the thin frame, the indeterminately mousy hair pulled back in a tidy French roll as usual. Once she was startled at the depth of colour and intelligence in the eyes, more green than hazel, when Miss Gray took her glasses off to clean them. They are beautiful eyes, with long lashes and delicately curved eyebrows, generally hidden by the thick plastic frames. She thinks how little she really knows about her, although she has been here, in the bookshop, as long as Paula has been in the town.

"You can go now if you like. We've done quite well today."

"Thanks. Shall I come in a bit earlier tomorrow to do the windows?"

"Oh no. There's no need."

It is Thursdays that the usual cleaner comes to do all the outsides of the windows in the street. Paula enjoys watching his dexterity with the brush and the rubber blade, swooping over the glass in great random sweeps that somehow never miss a patch. She likes to get the insides done before he comes so that they enjoy the full effect of gleaming glass.

She takes her bag and slips out the back to where her small car is parked. Gordon always keeps her supplied with reliable wheels for around town and short trips. Miss Gray's old Morris Minor, its original green nicely polished, is something else that never changes, distinctive around the town. She has turned down a number of offers as they become more rare, and she fully acknowledges that if they didn't have a particularly good garage man in the town she could probably not keep it going. He chases parts up at wreckers or even makes parts to fit when it needs servicing. Paula would like a more interesting car too, but Gordon has no faith in their reliability, so she drives around in the usual Japanese tin can and envies the solid frame of the old Morris.

As she drives home, to the house on the slopes of a hill at the edge of town, she remembers that she will not be cooking for Gordon tonight after all. It's Rotary night. So after her large lunch she only needs to boil an egg and not think of feeding anyone else. It's a relief to put her feet up in front of television, taking out Eleanor's letter to reread, while she dreams about it.

The door clunks shut and Gordon comes in. The letter is open in her lap.

"You haven't put the light on," he sounds surprised, as he flicks the switch. He's in as expansive a mood as his waistline, giving her the usual side on one-armed hug and kiss on the cheek as he passes. Then he tells her the habitual anecdote from the meeting, this time a funny story, followed by an incident from his working day.

When he asks about her day she does not give the usual non-committal answer. She looks at him, as if seeing him clearly for the first time in years. He hasn't changed much in that time, just a dusting of grey in the dark hair around his face, a thinning patch on top that she only sees when he's sitting at the table and she walks around him. It's a strong face with a decided nose and chin, and smile lines around the mouth and eyes. She hesitates, thoughtful, taking in the solidity and warmth of the man she has loved for sixteen years. The man she still loves. Doesn't she?

"I've got a letter from Eleanor. Remember her?"

Her too casual tone alerts him.

"Eleanor? That dizzy blonde you studied with? Thought she'd dropped off the edge of the world."

"Well she did in a way. She's written from London. Must be working there now."

"Ever marry and settle down?"

"No. I don't think so."

"What's she writing for so suddenly?"

12

"She's suggesting I go and visit her. She's got a place in France this summer and she wants me to come and stay."

"Wow. Just like that. Silence all these years, then come and stay in France." He looks at her, his expression unreadable. "Do you want to?"

She's startled at his directness.

"It would be nice to actually use some French."

"What about your job?"

"I should think I could take some time off," the idea is growing more attractive.

"I suppose there's nothing to keep you here now," he looks back at the television again.

What does he mean? Doesn't he care what she does? She can't speak again until the news is finished. Gordon hates being interrupted. She busies herself making tea, bringing it to him.

"Reckon you could still speak French?" He switches off after the weather.

"I'd like a chance to try."

"Don't know that I could trust you with all those French men!"

It doesn't seem the right moment to pursue the subject, as he follows her to bed with a gleam in his eye.

After they make love she lies awake, realising that they practically always make love on Rotary nights. What is it about men that they become amorous after a night out with other men? She can't remember ever feeling especially amorous after a night out with her woman friends. The Rotary Ladies' Nights she goes to do not seem to inspire particularly loving feelings. She notices the easy joking camaraderie of the men, their reminders to each other to 'keep it clean' because there are ladies present. Overall their meetings and rituals seem singularly boring to her. The one conference they attended together was rather fun though. The most enjoyable part was the extended hotel meals and the late night swims in bubbling shadowed hot pools. That was rather amorous, but then water always turns her on, especially in stimulating company.

Gordon has always lived in the same town, only leaving to study, then returning to go into his father's business. Paula's family became less rooted, less available.

She remembers taking her home for granted as a child, with her own room, her own parents who protected her from the scary world outside. When she went to school home remained her base. She saw the rest of the world in reference to it. However inadequate it might have been in comparison with other people's homes, and as she grew older she did make those comparisons, it was still hers. Even when she disparaged it, it was always a relief to get there.

Perhaps her parents did not realise what they did when they took it all away so suddenly. Even though she had left, was a university student of nineteen and only went home in the holidays, Paula could not believe how desolate she felt when her parents sold the house and went overseas. Instead of applying for academic posts in other schools, her father applied to other countries, and they vanished into South East Asia. They decided it was not worth the hassle of keeping the house now that both Paula and Stephen were studying in Auckland. There were plenty of relations to visit in the holidays, and already they were staying in the city for holiday work.

Suddenly there were no roots. The base was gone. It was hard not to attack her parents, not to voice her dismay and bewilderment, even her anger at not having been consulted. Her mother in particular was so bubbly and excited at the prospect of living somewhere else that Paula forced herself to smile and share in her expectations, hiding her glum expression as she looked at everything for the last time.

She felt a displaced person, an exile, and her mind balked at the fact that it was all so final. Even the fulfilment of their promises of holidays in exotic places seemed insufficient recompense to her.

Stephen was not nearly so bothered. Although he was a year younger he was happily settled in Auckland, doing well in his law studies, and already working part time for the law firm where he expected to get a job when he graduated. He took what he wanted and said the rest could be thrown away.

Paula could not say the same about her favourite books and treasured miniatures, her dolls' house furniture and the range of dolls and soft toys. She did not have room for them in the flat either, so they had to be stored, carefully packed into clearly labelled boxes, and gratefully reclaimed as soon as she had a home of her own.

It was not long after her parents left that she met Gordon at a casual friend's birthday party. He was so solid and reassuring. She realised years later that he probably represented the permanence and continuity that her parents removed from her life. She needed a home base, someone to turn to for comfort and support. Gordon made an admirable substitute.

Her father's sudden illness several years later, when Paula already had a baby, left her parents uprooted in a foreign country. They moved back to New Zealand and bought a small house in the same town where they used to live. Her father died not long after, leaving her mother to take up her life there again, at least with her own friends on hand. Gordon was the sterling rock of support for all of them, her brother Stephen as shattered as she was. What would she have done without Gordon all through the years?

In the morning Gordon looks at her as he eats his breakfast egg.

"Suppose you could do with a break. I can't get away," it's almost grudging.

"You mean I can go?" It seems unbelievable, as if she's been protecting herself from the dangers of travel by thinking he won't let her go anyway.

"Guess so. If you think she means it." He drinks his

coffee and leaves for work.

Paula is amazed. Paradoxically she starts to wonder if he wants to get rid of her, if he doesn't care what she does. Then she pulls herself together, telling herself not to be silly. She's going. She goes upstairs and pulls out an atlas in her work room to look for Concarneau. As she takes the atlas to the window for the light, she looks out over the town. There is a clear view of Rivertown from the top floor rooms of their home on the slopes, across the river at the bottom of the hill, its curves lazily looping the settlement, with bridges either side. It's a cosy compact place, lots of trees, no buildings taller than two stories high, just the ubiquitous New Zealand quarter acre sections with sprawling weather board or stucco homes. The newer developments on the hillside follow a similar pattern, even though the sections and houses may be a bit larger. There are quietly prosperous dairy farms on the river plains, the edges of which rise into native bush, or sheep country. The forests of exotic timbers, for which the indigenous bush was felled, are out of sight where the coast road goes inland again. It's a complacent sort of community. Paula's never really questioned it before. Her eyes go back to the map. She's quite sure French towns will be completely different. The thought is stimulating.

She puts down the atlas and goes to look at the calendar. When is the play on? Can she pull out and get away sooner? At least Easter is early. She couldn't leave before the children's holiday then, Emma's first break from boarding school. They'll just have to do without her for the next holidays. Paula loses herself in dreaming before she writes to Eleanor, ready to catch the post on her way to work.

16

Chapter Three

Dear Eleanor,

Well I can hardly believe it. You again, after all this time. Yes I am still here. Not as entirely rooted in domesticity and suburbia as you might think. The nice thing about small towns is that everyone makes their own fun. We have a good active local drama group and I've been both acting and directing in the last few years, with the children older.

They're both away at boarding school now, and I've been working part time in the bookshop here. Rather fun really, keeping up with a lot of the latest writing. Lots more New Zealand writers now, and very good too. I'm sure you'd find them interesting. Bet you've only ever heard of our Booker prize winner.

Anyway, yes, I'm coming. But I can't come till after the children's Easter holidays. I'm supposed to be in a local drama production soon too.

It all seems a bit unreal. Tell me about Concarneau. I've looked it up on the map. Should I fly into London or Paris? Where could you meet me more easily? Not sure if I could find my way to the Atlantic coast of Brittany alone, but maybe I could try.

This really is exciting. We went to a business conference in California three years ago, and we've been to Australia and several Pacific islands, but Europe.

A dream coming true, pal. Thanks.

They are rehearsing the play in Roz's large front room, and the words of Chekhov are ringing around the wooden panelling. Paula as Popova is shouting down Smirnov, calling him a bully and a bear, while he challenges her as a woman to be equal if she wants equal rights.

Paula loves the response, fire in her eyes and voice as she calls for her husband's pistols to fight a duel with the bully. Is it her imagination or is the flashing of Gareth's eyes as they look into hers more of a challenge than Chekhov requires?

They're all dissolving in laughter as Gareth overacts and then stumbles over the words. He makes a good Smirnov, the new Welsh school teacher with his dark good looks. It's fun playing opposite him.

"Very enlightened chap, old Chekhov, talking about women's rights and equality more than a hundred years ago," he stops laughing to speak.

"Ah but New Zealand was way ahead too. We gave women the vote in 1893. It was the centenary not long ago."

"Did you? All those pioneer women eh."

"Wonder what Chekhov would have thought of equal rights under communism." Ben draws them back to the play. He's a local farmer, just right for the farm worker role. The writing is so good that it flows easily, the parts seem to fall into place, the moves develop naturally. In two hours they go through it a number of times, with Roz making notes and diagrams. They reach saturation point. She goes to make coffee and call her husband Bill to join them. He's a local solicitor who was at school with Gordon, and like him, returned to work in the home town. The four of them have become close through the years, the two men obviously pleased that their wives are such good friends. Paula is fond of Bill, but she has never really thought about him as an individual, he is too good at melting into the background, the discreet grey man of law.

Gareth and Ben finish their coffee and get ready to

go.

"Can I give you a lift?" Gareth looks at Paula with his expressive eyes.

She laughs. "No thanks. I'm just down the road."

His glance lingers on her as they say good bye and leave. Is it a reproachful look?

"Funny man. What made him think I'd go with him?"

"Don't be so naïve. He's attracted to you." Bill's gaze is steady over his refill of coffee.

"But I'm married."

"That's no handicap in a small town like this."

"You missed your chance there," Roz joins in.

"You can't be serious."

"It all happens here." Bill turns away to rinse his mug.

"You should know. You handle all the divorces," Roz is laconic, needling.

"Good material for a play on small town life, actually." Bill ponders the idea.

"I'm sure it's been done," Paula dismisses it.

"We should write one together. Only you're about to take off." Roz sounds bitter.

"Off? Where are you off to?" Bill turns, curious.

"Whoops! She's off to France, lucky woman."

"Well it's not definite yet."

"You're only jealous," Bill takes Roz's mug too, giving her a hard look.

"Of course I'm jealous. Why can't I just take off to France?"

"You've been, remember. With me."

"That was ages ago."

Paula feels a bit embarrassed by the intensity of the exchange. She mumbles goodbye and leaves. Roz sees her off distractedly. What's going on? As she drives the brief journey home Paula thinks about Roz and Bill, then about Gareth. No harm in a bit of flirting but he couldn't be serious.

Gordon is still up, watching a documentary with some work spread out on the coffee table. Paula immediately tells him about Gareth, the flirting, the invitation.

"I'd better watch out, all these glamorous Romeos you play with."

"Bill reckons it goes on all the time here."

"Don't be so innocent. You lead such a sheltered life with Miss Gray."

"She doesn't gossip if that's what you mean."

"I bet Roz does."

"She just tells stories for fun."

"Listen next time. And what about Ben?"

"Ben?"

"Bet he didn't say anything about Barbara's taking off."

"You don't mean it."

"Rumour has it she's not coming back."

"You're joking."

"Rumour also has it she left because she found him in the guest room with one of her guests."

"I don't believe you."

"He's got a bit of a reputation in the bars, has Ben."

Paula is stunned. How unobservant has she been? How come Gordon knows so much?

The next day is Wednesday, so she meets Roz for lunch in the coffee bar. Roz comes in looking rather belligerent.

"We didn't get on to dates last night. When are you going?"

"Not sure. I'm pencilled in straight after Easter."

"Well the play's important. You've got to fit round that."

Paula is surprised. She makes a mild response while she thinks about Roz's attitude. "What's the date of the play then?"

"I'm meeting with the producers of the other two tonight to decide whether we do it before or after Easter."

"I'll be here for the kids over Easter, but I want to

leave straight after that."

"But I don't think the plays will be ready before then."

"Well if you want me you might have to talk them into it."

They glare at each other over their salad rolls. Paula can't believe it. They don't normally argue. What's wrong with Roz?

"I don't think there's a hope Gareth will know his lines in time if it's too soon."

"He won't want to make a fool of himself. He'll do it whatever time it is."

"Yes, I suppose he is rather vain," Roz concedes the point but not the argument. They finish lunch uneasily.

"I don't want to leave going any later. Maybe you should take my part."

"No. I want to produce this one. I'll see what the others say." Roz would promise no more.

Paula returns to work a little shaken. Why is Roz pushing it? Is it jealousy? It's hardly her fault she's been invited to France. She remembers Roz talking about the time she and Bill travelled together, just after their marriage. Bill had spent a year at Oxford so there were lots of English friends to entertain them. Roz moaned once that it was a waste going to so many romantic places with a husband in tow, although Paula thought that should be romantic in itself, as newly marrieds. Perhaps that's it, Roz envies her freedom in going without Gordon. Silly really. What difference will it make? She'll be with Eleanor. She dismisses Roz from her mind and concentrates on work.

Her thoughts are hard to pin down though, as the afternoon is not very busy. They fly to Eleanor, to the past, to all they once shared. There will be freedom in joining Eleanor, a freedom she hasn't considered before. Has she ever really broken out, except with Eleanor? It always seemed so daring, going off with her to student parties, shows, poetry readings. She remembers the time she was persuaded to read one of her own poems, her trembling excitement, moist fear, quivering voice. It was quite well received but she never wanted to repeat the performance, her poems too private for such exposure.

Eleanor had no such qualms. No illusions about her poetry either, which she claimed was totally derivative of McGonagall doggerel. She would have people falling off their chairs with laughter as she dead panned her send-ups of the university and virtually everyone they knew. Her sense of humour, her sense of adventure, always drew people to her, widening her circle of friends. Paula's too, as Eleanor was loyal, dragging her off whether she wanted or no.

Now she's being 'dragged off' again by Eleanor's excitement, her rush of enthusiasm. But not reluctantly. Not at all. She realises now how much she's missed that enthusiasm. How much involvement with family and life in a small town has absorbed all her energy, making her forget there ever was another side to her life.

Well there was. She's going to find it again. Regardless of Roz, Gordon, play, or anything else, she's going to find Eleanor again. She can't wait.

"Paula!" Miss Gray's voice calls her back to help deal with the after school rush.

Miss Gray's not looking very well, she thinks afterwards, offering to make more coffee once the shop empties. Miss Gray sits gratefully as Paula boils the kettle and rinses their mugs. She wonders if her boss ever travelled, what she did before coming to Rivertown and her life in the shop.

"I'd like to take two or three months off this winter," she says suddenly, making it all definite at once. "Would you be able to manage without me?"

Miss Gray's eyes turn to her, seeming to take it in with difficulty.

"Yes, I dare say. Not having another baby are you?"

Paula laughs. "Not when I've just got my two away to school and started enjoying my freedom. No, a friend has invited me to join her in France. I'd like to go."

"Yes of course. You must take the opportunity."

"Have you ever been to France?" Paula seizes the moment, curious.

"Yes. A long time ago. It will be very different now." Miss Gray puts down her mug, then goes out into the shop.

Paula knows there is a friend of Miss Gray's who used to help out. She's retired, but still returns when Paula takes holidays, so there shouldn't be any problem.

Nora, Gordon's mother, is quite friendly with Miss Gray. That evening they're around at her place for dinner, so Paula takes the chance to question her.

"No, she's never mentioned travel," Nora pauses in handing around vegetables. "But I've never asked."

Paula reads a slight rebuke in the statement. One shouldn't ask, in Nora's world. She lets it go for the moment. She likes Nora. She's an easy mother-in-law. She's stayed elegant and well dressed ever since Paula first visited as a poor student. She originally felt self conscious, but never unwelcome. Nora is warm and generous, she genuinely likes people and keeps open house. She's also an indulgent but practical grandmother, who never interferes but is always available in a crisis. She's always been the same, both before and after the death of her beloved Joseph when Paula's children were quite small. It is sad that they do not remember much about the adoring grandfather who relaxed and spoilt them in a way he never had his own sons. Gordon only got to know his father through working with him those last few years, his other brothers having left to study, then work in dentistry and architecture in the cities. He's never talked much about his father, but Paula knows how much he misses him, how in a sense he still works for him, expanding the business, showing him all over again how well he manages it. She's sure Nora realises this when she shows more than normal appreciation for Gordon's changes, saying how pleased and proud his father would have been. She's a perceptive woman. Paula feels she's never really appreciated her sufficiently.

"Paula's going to desert me this winter," Gordon announces over the apple pie. Paula wishes he wouldn't put it like that. Nora looks startled.

"Just for a holiday," Paula puts in hastily. "A friend's invited me to join her in France."

"Oh I'm so glad," Nora is instantly generous. "You'll have a chance to use all your French, and it will be such a nice time of year to go there. Summer in France," her eyes are dreamy.

"She's joining some dizzy blonde she studied with," Gordon seems determined to be negative.

Paula finds herself telling Nora all about Eleanor, and how much she wants to see her again. Gordon is sidelined in the discussion, Nora becoming enthusiastic on her behalf, making all sorts of suggestions, even offering to help prepare her wardrobe for travel, to go shopping if necessary.

"I'd love to get Miss Gray talking about where she went in France," she returns to her boss almost without thinking.

Nora is pensive, she must have been wrong in thinking her critical.

"In all the time I've known her she's never mentioned it. But then, she must have been close to forty when she came here, so that's half a life time of activities we know nothing about."

"She doesn't talk about herself, does she."

"I expect she thinks no-one would be interested. She likes a quiet, unfussy life. I think she's content enough, in her own way."

"Probably got an ex husband and several kids tucked away somewhere," Gordon butts in again.

"Nonsense," his mother is brisk. "I suppose I'll have to feed you in your wife's absence, since you never would learn to cook."

"Of course I can cook! You women all think you're indispensable. I'll do very well on my own."

"You're good at scrambled eggs," Paula admits.

24

They take coffee away from the table. Paula is not allowed to do anything in the kitchen, Nora insists she relax here, a working woman. At least she has a woman come to help several times a week so Paula doesn't feel quite so guilty.

On the way home she suggests to Gordon that it would make things easier if he did let Nora cook for him a bit.

"I'd really rather not. Don't I deserve some time to myself too?"

"Well yes," Paula is put out, she hasn't thought of it like that, time out for Gordon as well, but it's fair enough, she decides.

"So long as you eat properly then, not all takeaways."

"You women are all the same. Scared I'll lose weight?"

"More likely I'll put it on with that great sounding French food."

"Not if you rely on Eleanor's cooking you won't."

"Fancy your remembering that. She might have learnt by now."

"Doesn't sound like it. Flitting around on expense accounts."

"How on earth will I fit into her world, I'm so small town."

"Don't worry about it, she's taking time out from it."

"Maybe she's homesick for an old friend."

"You certainly used to talk all night when you did see her."

"I guess that won't have changed."

There are times, by sudden contrast, when Gordon seems to find it all, find her, a bit exciting. When they get home he notices the map of France she's put up on the kitchen wall.

"It's certainly given you a sparkle, thinking about France," he puts his arms around her as she puts the dish of food Nora insisted on giving her into the fridge.

"Will you really manage all right without me?"

"Of course. I did go flatting as a student remember."

"Yes but it was Colin who cooked the Sunday roasts."

"Those were the days. All the girlfriends coming on Sundays."

"Like the Sunday roast at the hostel before we went flatting."

"Remember Mattie in the kitchen?"

"She used to cook us up an omelette if the late dinners were crawling with cockroaches."

"Ugh. Don't remember that bit."

"Men have such selective memories."

"Sensible. Only remember the good bits."

She looks at her sensible Gordon and lets him take her upstairs to bed and make love to her. He's good and kind, she will miss him, awfully.

Chapter Four

Dear Polly,

Wow! Just like that indeed! Must admit I never thought you'd make it. Always ready to try the long shot though.

Come to London. Early to mid April would be wonderful. Good thing Easter's so early this year. You can have an English spring. You've never been. Can't believe anyone has never been these days. We can finish April in Paris. Where are those stars you used to have in your eyes when we talked about that, old pal? Get them ready. April in Paris is bliss, umbrellas and all.

Then we'll get a car and drive to Brittany, down the Loire Valley, all those castles, you know. We can take several days. You're getting me all excited at being able to show the place to absolutely new eyes. Jaded old me, actually getting excited. Hang it all, we're still the right side of forty, a bit longer anyway. So let's make the most of it. You won't believe how wide your horizons will become away from the Bay. This is our prime, Polly. We can have so much fun. Guess I really have been getting jaded. What I need is to see things through new eyes, your eyes, so it doesn't all seem as pointless as it has lately.

Oh the job's been great, till the boss got the usual ideas. I'm probably getting, or got, to the age and time when jobs won't be so easy, but hang it all, I'm still restless, still not ready to settle. And certainly sick of being anyone's bit *on the side while he stays safely married, which is what it's all about. So time out in France is well overdue.*

Maybe I'll get so used to vegetating I'll buy a place there, rusticate and get fat on French pastry and write a novel. Time for a change. But then it always was for me. How about you? Gordon and small town domesticity must have got to you in some ways by now.

Start looking out your background on Britain and France, and anywhere else in Europe. Decide what you most want to see and do. Great shows in London. Time for everything. And it's all so close here. Roman ruins, sun soaked Riviera, Swiss Alps and lakes, castles in Spain, all the tourist clichés are on tap. We can fit it all in if you like. Or just stay quietly and soak up French ambience and seafood, wine and cheeses. Hey I'm getting excited again myself. Have to watch it or I'll lose the blasé image. Can't have that.

Gee pal I'm so thrilled you're coming. Did I say that? It'll be like old times. They may say you can never go back, but I find that basically people don't change all that much, and the Polly I know is still in there, ready to break out. Set her free pal. I'm waiting.

YoP,
Nell

Eleanor posts her letter to Paula on her way to the Waldorf Brasserie. She's thoughtful as she gives the hotel doorman her car keys. What will Paula be like after all this time? The same rather unadventurous friend, the one who opted for marriage and children in a small town? She can't have changed all that much or she wouldn't still be there, surely. She catches sight of Martin in the foyer, waiting for her. Bother Martin for always being early, no time to sit and think, just the rush from work to catch an early meal before this play everyone's talking about.

"You look tired," his greeting is not flattering.

"I am."

He takes her arm solicitously and they go through to the busy brasserie. She tries to discourage him, not feeling nearly as decrepit as he seems to think. Besides, he doesn't own her, as his possessive arm seems to be saying. In fact, he never will.

The street doors are closed to the cool March air. She gives up her coat and scarf, absentmindedly watching Martin shed his, revealing his anonymous business suit and discreet tie, another faceless city man from the stockbroker belt. His latest car will already be valet parked. She doesn't let him pick her up, preferring the independence of her own modest wheels. As they're seated she asks herself what she ever saw in him. Maybe she won't see him again. Leaving London seems a better idea every day.

Martin fusses about wine, orders her duck and salad with a minimum of consultation. He knows too much about her when he even orders her food, she thinks.

"Do you know the background to the play?" he asks. Naturally he's done his homework.

"It's a journalist in the war," she doesn't bother to enlarge.

He does. "Bit more than that. What do you know about the Potsdam Conference and Clement Atlee?"

"Lots." How dare he quiz her. "We did study history in the colonies you know." She lets herself become amused that he's so ready to launch into a lecture.

"Oh," he's almost put out, but she knows he's unstoppable.

"And Michael Gambon's Tom Driburgh, so it should be good," she adds. She doesn't want to talk about the play, she'd rather just enjoy it. She doesn't want to be here with Martin any more either.

He's only momentarily silenced. He launches into an analysis of the stock market and Eleanor switches to polite listening mode, the odd smile or nod, while her mind drifts. Just behind Martin's left ear, the rather sensual whorl her tongue has discovered previously, a large woman is complaining loudly about London traffic. Beyond her is a woman in the corner, thin and elegant, with a little of the appearance of Paula as Eleanor remembers her. Same straight brown hair and large eyes in a narrow face, but she's erect and confident in a way Paula never was. She's wearing Dior and diamonds too, and her partner is definitely city. Eleanor puts her arms back and lifts the weight of her mass of blonde hair off the collar of her neat dark business suit. She's looking far too city herself, but there wasn't time to change. Perhaps she'll have her hair cut. It's feeling rather heavy for the summer. Maybe a new look for Paula would be a good idea.

The food comes. The waiter pours more wine. Martin looks at his watch. Eleanor smiles to herself and eats her duck with pleasure. The food is good here. The bareness of wood and glass in the brasserie suits her mood.

When they walk the short distance around the curving road to the Aldwych Theatre Martin is still talking. Naturally he has the tickets. Eleanor feels detached, is distant with her escort. Several other people from the Brasserie are in the foyer of the theatre. They have good seats, and as always, she enjoys the rustle of excitement as the theatre fills, looking to see if the boxes are in use, if the balconies are filling too. At least Martin is silent once the curtain goes up. They're both absorbed in the action on stage, the edge of real history unfolding holds everyone's attention.

It is impossible to talk in the interval, in the crowded noisy bar where Martin queues for drinks and Eleanor is hailed by several people she knows. Unavoidable. She's been here too long. Martin is doing his usual networking, scanning the crowd for likely people and darting off to make an impression. How tedious. She's pleased when the bells ring and they can forget everything but the actors for a bit longer.

Martin insists on supper and a post mortem on the play.

"There's that new one on art, you know, a modern piece and whether it's worth anything. Shall I make a booking for next week?"

"No thanks. I'm disengaging."

"From art? London? me?" Martin's normally well modulated tones rise a little, as do his eyebrows. Eleanor suspects he plucks them, they're so straight.

"All three, I think. Clean sweep time."

"You're leaving?"

"Yes."

"When?"

"After Easter. Job finishes, time to clear out for a while."

"Where are you going?" Martin is genuinely surprised. He can't conceive of life outside London, has never shown any curiosity about what Eleanor might have done before he met her. He's not interested in her origins, apart from the occasional colonial crack.

"Friend's place in France. Brittany."

Martin gives an audible shudder. Soon he'll be relieved she's going. Anyone who likes the French and wants to go to France is simply not part of his comprehension.

"You'll be back."

"I don't think so." She shrugs and finishes her coffee.

He looks at her, full in the eyes this time.

"A last fling then?" It's an invitation. He would have made it regardless, but it's become a little poignant now and she doesn't want any part of it.

"Don't feel you need to. It's so complicated with both our cars," she tries to give him an easy let out, but he won't be deterred.

"We must at least make a decent farewell. I'll bring you back to your car in the morning." He's determined to do the right thing, to fulfill some role he needs to play in her life before he leaves it.

31

"Oh never mind, Martin. We've done it all, there's no need to back track. Let's just say goodbye."

He detects the trace of acid impatience she's trying to conceal and looks hurt. Then she looks at the whorl of his ear again and relents a little, feeling sorry for him.

"I suppose you can come back to my flat for a nightcap, but no staying over. I need my sleep."

He's mollified but subdued. As she gets her car and drives off she hopes he won't follow, but she knows he will. It's not far to Bloomsbury. She takes her park and locks the car, going up to the flat. Martin will have to find a place for his car. He's only a few minutes after her, hardly time to breathe, she thinks as she lets him in.

She gets the glasses and Benedictine. She knows his tastes. Then she tries to detach her mind as he makes love to her, knowing it won't take long, and this will be the last time. She enjoys it despite all. He knows how to bring her on, another of his careful skills, his considerate love making. She stifles a laugh and lets go. Maybe there will even be times when she misses him, but she rather doubts it.

Chapter Five

Dear Eleanor,

I'm getting nervous. I've never travelled on my own before. It's a long flight straight through but apparently I can get a shower and walk around in the airport at Singapore.

It'll be good to see you in London. Hope there's no bombings going on this year. That scares me, but guess everyone just goes on living normal lives. Not much else you could do I suppose. Gee Eleanor do you still even look the same? Hair colour? Size? Don't think I've changed much. Put on a bit of weight after the kids but I've been swimming and exercising lately so I'm quite fit. Given up trying new hairstyles and gone back to the same one. You won't miss me in the crowd.

What kind of clothes will I need? All my work ones seem so shabby at the thought of Europe. Nora has offered to go on a buying trip to Auckland with me, which should be fun.

The kids are already putting in orders for what they want from London and Paris. I'm not committing myself to anything. This is my trip. It all seems so amazing still. Should be writing to you in French to try it out and see if I can. Suppose yours is as fluent as ever. It's going to take a bit of time for me. I'm listening to tapes though, trying to talk French in my head, and reading as much as I can.

Remember Dr Frost at University? How we had to climb up those stairs in the old clock tower to his office for our oral exam, and he would

admire our tans and offer us chocolate biscuits,
and how I ran around the other side of the stair
well when he touched my arm once afterwards.
Such a scared little rabbit I was. Still feel a bit
that way sometimes at the prospect of the big
wide world.
Don't worry. Nothing is going to put me off this
trip. Fear of flying, bombs, crowds, nothing.
Europe here I come.
YoP,
Polly.

It's satisfying to sign her name Polly again. As if she's
already turned back the clock and become the younger
unencumbered Paula once more. Gordon doesn't like
diminutives, which is partly why they called the
children such definite incorruptible names as Simon
and Emma. Even she winces when she hears school
mates say Si or Em, but fortunately those forms never
seem to stick. But Polly. It's an affectionate name. She
likes it.

At work she's unpacking a box of books when Miss
Gray comes into the stock room. She's quite chatty
today, even mentioning Paula's trip and asking her
where she hopes to go.

Paula is pleased to be able to talk about it. She
wonders how old Miss Gray is. She always looks and
sounds the same, as if her whole life has been spent
in this particular bookshop, even though she knows it
hasn't been. Small and neat, she often makes Paula feel
big and clumsy. Her greying hair is so smoothly
controlled it makes Paula conscious of her own long
hair that resists all attempts to keep it in any kind of
restraint. Still, she long ago decided she doesn't suit
short hair, and Gordon likes it long. Too fine and wispy
though, she always envied the thick abundance of
Eleanor's hair, with which she could do anything she
liked. Miss Gray's is fine too. How does she keep it so
tidy? No sign of any spray or mousse either. Her

thoughts are called back to the shop.

"Would you like to visit a bookshop in London? I could arrange the contact."

"Yes please. I'd love to."

"Perhaps even a publishing house."

"Did you know any?"

"Well, I had a small book taken by one once."

"You wrote a book?" Paula is excited, amazed.

"It's nothing. Just a travel journal."

"Really? Where did you go?"

"We did an overland train trip from China to London." Miss Gray is brief, brisk, not encouraging.

"Where is it? Could I read it?"

"No no. It's all out of date." Miss Gray is dismissive, reluctant. Paula bites her lip, trying to think of a way to persuade her.

"Have you ever sold it in the shop?"

"Oh no. People here wouldn't want to read it." Miss Gray obviously regrets having spoken. The subject is closed, there are people in the shop.

Paula finds it hard to imagine the Miss Gray she knows writing a book. Even less can she see her travelling on the Trans-Siberian railway. But there is a tradition of strong taciturn English women making such unlikely journeys in history. There's no reason why Miss Gray shouldn't be another one.

Paula tries to return to the subject later, but Miss Gray refuses to discuss it, either convinced that Paula wouldn't like it, or trying to hide it altogether. She's not going to learn any more that way, but she's not going to let it go either.

It's later in the week when Miss Gray asks her to mind the shop for the afternoon as she has an appointment in the next town. She doesn't explain, just leaves when Paula gets back from lunch, giving Paula the key and asking her to lock up, then drop the key in during the evening.

It's not busy for the first hour or two, and after some dusting she settles in the work room with the door open and the mirror angled to see if anyone comes into the shop. It's the chance she's been waiting for, and she starts a systematic search of the shelves and cupboards. She's not very hopeful, thinking Miss Gray's not likely to keep her book in the shop if she doesn't want anyone to see it.

The shelves yield nothing she hasn't seen before. She starts on Miss Gray's desk, feeling a bit guilty but still determined. The bottom drawer seems to be locked, but it's only stiff from lack of use. Under a pile of papers are several old books. One of them is a small black hardback, with a photograph let into the cover. It's a photograph of Lake Baikal. She pulls it out just as she glimpses someone coming into the shop. There's time to see the title, 'A Traveller's Notebook' by Virginia Gray, before she hides it in her bag and goes out. Dare she take it home, and if she does will she get a chance to return it while Miss Gray is at lunch tomorrow? She decides to take the risk.

At the end of the afternoon, having stayed the extra hour to keep the shop open, she carefully checks everything, taking the till records in a bag for Miss Gray. Then she locks up, driving to the supermarket first to get something quick and easy for the evening meal. Miss Gray's place is only a small detour on her way home, a wooden cottage near the river in one of the areas first developed by settlers many years ago. She has always admired the white painted cottage, its lattice work on the front verandah, with climbing vines and hanging baskets, the garden between the house and the white fence where Miss Gray has planted cottage flowers and herbs where other people would have grass. The section is just big enough for a driveway down the side to a garage, a later addition. Miss Gray has planted wisteria and other vines to almost entirely cover its out of place iron. The garage door is open and Paula can see the Morris inside. Miss Gray is back.

She opens the gate and walks up the path, thick lavender bushes either side. As she reaches the steps she sees Miss Gray is sitting in her battered wicker chair on the verandah, barely visible behind the white railing. Her eyes are closed. It is so unusual to see Miss Gray sitting doing nothing that Paula pauses on the first step. Miss Gray looks so peaceful. Every other time she's called Miss Gray has been busy in the garden, or bustling around her neat kitchen, her two sleek well fed and groomed cats always close by. Darcy, the haughty grey with a white bib, is curled up in her lap, while Heathcliff, the black one, is stretched out on the top step. Paula steps over him and Miss Gray's eyes open.

"There you are. Thank you for staying on for me," Miss Gray straightens her glasses and rises, the cat jumping off her lap.

"Don't get up," Paula's words are unheeded and she is taken inside for a small glass of sherry.

The living room is comfortable but quite impersonal. There are many books, a few pieces of good china, some engravings and good prints hanging from the old wooden picture rail running around the walls, and that is all, no photographs or memorabilia. The furniture is well worn, a kauri dresser the only piece of obvious value. Paula sits by the window in the upright winged chair where she has sat before. Miss Gray gives her the sherry glass and sits in the other winged chair by the fire place, with the reading table beside it holding her glasses case and a pile of books. There is a hand woven throw on the wooden settle against the wall, more books or literary magazines on the scatter of other small tables. The kauri floor boards show the gleam of polish, and the faded Persian carpet in tones of red is soft under foot, picking up the lighter tones of red in the striped pattern of the wall paper.

The distinguishing feature of this room is flowers. There are flowers from Miss Gray's garden on every available ledge or surface, from small posies of lavender and violets to a striking display of large blooms and greenery on its own table in the window nook. A spike of gladioli is nearly touching Paula's cheek. Most of the flowers are fresh, but some are dried arrangements. Miss Gray dries them herself, from a series of rafters and pulleys in her garage.

The black cat has already leaped on to Paula's knees, purring voluptuously as she strokes him.

She gives Miss Gray the key and the papers from the shop, telling her about the afternoon, which was fairly quiet. Miss Gray does not tell her anything about her trip away, only referring to the amount of commuter traffic on the road between Rivertown and the next bigger town as she drove back.

Paula turns down a second sherry, it's not a drink she enjoys very much, but she cannot leave until Miss Gray has picked her an aromatic spray of flowers from the garden. There is only ever one small vase of flowers on the window ledge in the back room of the book shop. Miss Gray keeps them freshly replaced, but she has never brought in more than the one simple posy, nor put them out in the shop itself.

As she drives off Paula reflects that it's a pleasant simple life Miss Gray leads, with her flowers and books and cats. Rather lonely though. She's not sure cats would be sufficient company for herself, but then, she's never lived on her own and she can't imagine that either. At least Miss Gray does get involved in town life with people like Nora, and Florence from the flower shop.

It's not until later, after dinner, that she has a chance to get away by herself while Gordon watches television. Miss Gray's book, a reproach in her bag in the car while she called on its writer, has not been out of her impatient thoughts all evening.

Paula handles the little book with care, taking it out to read avidly from cover to cover. It's good. It's even exciting. Miss Gray has quite a knack with words, and she evokes the atmosphere of her travels well, by local buses, trains, the Trans-Siberian Railway.

'My friend had fortunately purchased a samovar in Vladivostok, so we were able to make tea on the train.

As advised we were carrying plenty of snack foods. The other people in our compartment were very polite and gentle. A family group of three generations. We did a lot of smiling and nodding and pointing at things by way of communication. The little girl liked to sit beside me and look at the pictures in the travel book I was reading. She would chatter away to her parents and point at the photographs.

'At one station we tried to ask about food, and my friend was taken by the hand and lead on to the platform to visit the little stalls. They brought back enough hot food for everyone and it was much more tasty than the tinned and dried stuff we'd been having. After that we joined them several times until they left the train at Omsk. There was much more smiling and hand clasping as they took all their bundles down from the racks and heaped them on the platform. I gave the little girl my travel book, and she hugged it to her chest, still holding it and waving as the train moved off. We had the compartment to ourselves for a while, until we were closer to Moscow when it filled again.'

Paula skims the pages, devouring each episode, frequently rereading pieces and relating them to the central section of photographs. The photographs are only of places, no figures in them except the population of occasional busy streets or stations. Certainly no Europeans in the early sections of the journey.

'We decided to make a detour to Vienna. My friend had always wanted to see the horses of the Spanish Riding School, while I wanted to see the Schönbrunn Palace for myself. We were not disappointed. We found a modest room overlooking a park, and were able to walk nearly everywhere, or use the local buses. Vienna is wonderfully compact for the walker. We will never forget the cafés either, the cakes and pastries that are so different from anywhere else in the world. We both put on weight in spite of the walking, and decided it was as well we were not staying any longer.'

In the centre section Paula finds several photographs

of Vienna, one with a figure in front of the palace that might be Miss Gray, but it's a bit too distant. She returns to the pages of the book.

'There was a silly incident in Paris when my hat blew off while we were walking along the Seine. There was a tourist boat passing at the time, and the wind lifted it over the side of the boat and a man on top reached up and caught it. He waved it towards us and then gestured to the wharf where the boat would soon be stopping. It was on the other side of the river and some distance away so we just waved it away and shook our heads. He promptly put my hat on his rather large head to show his friends, my little straw boater on this great big man making us laugh aloud. His friends were obviously very amused too, but they were moving quite quickly and we couldn't see what happened after that. I put my scarf around my head instead, and we bought several books and engravings from the bouquinistes by the river. We were still standing looking at a series of old postcards when the man came up to us with my hat! I couldn't believe it. Nothing would do but I had to put it back on my head to show him how pleased I was. He was Scandinavian I think, very blond and tall, and he had only a few words of English. The hat was a little stretched but it was a relief not to have to spend time looking for another.'

So that engraving of an old church over Miss Gray's mantelpiece is part of her journey too, thinks Paula. She is stunned by the cumulative effects of the descriptions. She never thought Miss Gray had it in her. Then she looks at it again, glances through and thinks more about the travelling companion Miss Gray always refers to as her 'friend'. No, there really is nothing to identify the sex of that 'friend'. She has only been assuming it was female. Her romantic mind dreams up all sorts of fantasies to add to Miss Gray's voyage.

It's quite a mystery, and Paula decides she's going to find out who Miss Gray's travelling companion was and what happened. There's a life and vivacity in the way she describes her travels that seem to have completely gone from the woman Paula knows. What was she like twenty five years ago when the book was published in London? What made her come back to such a small town, take over the bookshop?

All Paula knows is that about twenty years ago, with what she describes as a small legacy, Miss Gray bought the bookshop. She runs it well, keeps it up to date, keeps the magazine racks full for the town's browsers, generally merges into the main street. She has joined several organisations, works on committees with Nora, liaises closely with the library and the small museum. That's it. No evidence of any relations, any past.

Paula suspects she's probably letting her imagination run away with her, that if she asks Miss Gray's friendly neighbour, or somebody similarly straight forward, the whole mystery will be solved, proving not to be any sort of secret at all. She thinks not however, choosing to keep her thoughts to herself.

The next morning she arrives for work with the book in her bag, feeling guilty but partly satisfied. Miss Gray goes off to the bank and lunch as usual. When there's a lull Paula pulls the drawer open and puts the book back, as nearly as she can to the way it was. She's reluctant to let it go, but there's no way she can see of keeping it, especially now it's been mentioned. Miss Gray returns and the day goes on. Over tea in the afternoon Paula can't help asking about Europe again.

"Wouldn't you like to go back?" she asks Miss Gray, finding it hard to imagine how anyone, after the travels described in the book, could settle forever in a small town, as if nothing had happened.

"No. I'd rather remember it as it was for me. Nothing stays the same."

It's a perceptive remark. Paula understands the slight wistfulness of tone before Miss Gray closes her lips firmly and turns back to her desk.

Florence from the flower shop next door comes in. She talks to Miss Gray about a petition the shop owners are getting up against a new car park extension near the supermarket. It would mean pulling down an old fruit shop and taking over a small pleasant park, where lots of people sit with their shopping before walking home. Old men and women talk to each other in the sun, or mothers watch their children play. The only other park, though bigger and with a children's playground, is much further away from the shops. So most of the business people want to keep the status quo, and force the supermarket, if they do want more car park, to extend into the swampy area in another direction, which will obviously cost more.

"It's not as if they can't afford it, the money they turn over," Florence sounds a bit rueful. Her business as the only florist shop does reasonably well, but she's noticing a change since the supermarket went up, then started having cut flowers in the vegetable department.

"I do agree," Miss Gray is busy signing. Paula adds her name too.

Florence is famous for her flowered flowing dresses and picture hats, lavishly decorated with more flowers. It seems appropriate to have a slightly eccentric flower lady in town. She's always involved with everything that happens in the main centre, taking a keen interest in how the town looks. It's Florence who writes to the Council and the newspaper when the public flower-beds or road verges are neglected, often prodding them into action. Her own garden is a show place, people come from other towns to see it. She even uses some of her flowers in the shop. People wonder how she finds time for it all, but she never stops. At least her placid barman husband does the heavy work for her.

Before going home, Paula pops next door to buy a big bunch of flowers. Her own garden doesn't produce the profusion of colour that Florence manages, and Gordon is only interested in vegetables. She protests at the generous discount, but Florence is adamant. They all look after each other in the street, and sometimes Paula wonders how anyone manages to make a profit.

Unfortunately the new supermarket is changing things.

Chapter Six

Dear Polly,

So good to hear your voice the other day. See, I am actually at home quite a lot if you keep trying! You sound just the same.

Chekhov indeed. Who's playing opposite you, anyone thrilling? It's a great play, I saw it here a few years back, but you sure need the right person to make the sparks fly. Are school teachers there really that stimulating?

So Nora is helping you buy clothes. Has she good taste? I don't really remember much about her. You're going to strike very changeable weather in spring so you'll need removable layers, plus a coat, an all weather one would be fine. It will certainly rain a bit. Then later, just casual cottons, pants, for the coast. We'll be swimming.

Don't worry too much though. We can always get clothes here, might be more interesting for you than stuff from home. Don't load yourself up with too much luggage, it can be a curse. Travel light, says she who has never yet really succeeded in doing so!

Your timing is perfect. I finish this last job just after Easter. It's nearly here, for goodness sake. The daffodils are coming out in the London parks, tulips in window boxes. There'll be even more in France. I just love spring. All the bright colours after a bleak grey winter. Such obvious changes in seasons here, without all the winter greens and flowers of good old NZ. I love this rush of blood to the head, the newborn feeling

bursting out all over with the birds.
Goodness, I'm getting lyrical. Better watch it or
I'll break out in poetry and shock poor old
McGonagall again. You'll be here soon. Wow.
Can't wait. Bon voyage!
Je t'embrasse,
YoP
Nell

It's Saturday morning and Eleanor is doing research in the British Library. A letter from France has asked her to check out some photographic history. The writer is one person for whom she will drop everything to fulfil a request. There are not many people she would do that for. In fact, thinking about it, this is probably the only person she would respond to instantly.

To maximise her time, she has arranged to lunch with a friend who works in the Rare Manuscripts room of the library. She expects to make it another farewell before leaving for France. This is a date that will probably extend into the afternoon, a leisurely seduction once again. She sighs. After peeling off Martin should she peel off Nat as well? Perhaps it's a good idea to unclutter her life totally, leave London with no lingering ties. At least Martin in the City and Nat in the Library have never crossed paths. Her life so often falls into unconnected compartments. She likes it that way. It's been a good method of avoiding commitment, making it easy to move on, drop out, when she has the urge.

The morning goes quickly. It always does in the library, it's so easy to be side tracked, to carry on research into things not directly connected. The pile of requested books beside her grows, but by lunch time they've all been transferred to the other side to return, and her notebook has several pages of notes she hopes will be what is needed. Her mind is filled with much more irrelevant but fascinating data, about early photographers exploring in Africa. She's never really wanted to go to Africa, vast expanses of unpopulated land and wild animals not being to her taste, but some of the vivid descriptions she's just been reading make it sound rather attractive. Or perhaps it was only attractive all those years ago, not now.

Eleanor closes the last book and sorts the paper slips before taking the pile to the return desk. She looks around the big domed room, the shelves arcing above her right around the walls. Soon all the books will be gone, the library moved to new modern premises. It's sad to think of so many years of history and atmosphere ending, the beautiful reading room no longer being used in the same way. It makes her oddly sentimental for a moment. Another aspect of old London changing.

She's still waiting in the queue when Nat comes up beside her, already free for the day. He looks like the bibliophile he is, tall and thin, gold rimmed glasses, slightly stooped as if he spent his life bending over books, which he does. He has delicate hands with long sensitive fingers. His relaxation outside work is piano playing, anything from classics to jazz. He even helps out on piano in a jazz club some nights, he's that good. Eleanor often goes when he's playing, she can't resist dancing to the beat, letting herself go in the dim smoky club with a group of friends. She wonders if she can disengage while still staying friends, returning for jazz. But then, will she ever move back to London? Possibly not, so it doesn't matter.

By mutual consent they avoid both the staff cafeteria and the crowded weekend museum cafés. There's still a queue of tourists for the museum in the entry, waiting to have their bags searched.

Nat leads her to a well known courtyard wine bar, down a street opposite the museum. There are big concrete planters in the enclosed square, and sparrows seek crumbs under the tables outside. It's not warm enough yet, although several hardy people in coats and mufflers are braving the fresh air and thin sunshine. They go inside and down the stairs, where it's all dark wood and solid furniture.

"I'm going off to France for the summer," Eleanor announces over her pasta.

"Lucky you. I've only three weeks off, and Mother wants me to go on a Mediterranean cruise with her to meet heiresses."

"Most people would think that was even luckier."

"Not me," he sighs. His mother is a wealthy widow, who still tries to organise his life. She's been trying to find him a suitable bride to produce an heir for some years. Eleanor doesn't think Nat is the marrying kind. He's too much the scholar. His flat is meticulously kept, every one of the many books, manuscripts and artefacts in its place. No woman could ever meet his high standards, she's sure. Certainly no child would be welcome among his treasures.

"You could visit in Brittany. I've got a New Zealand friend coming. Not an heiress."

"Thanks but no. I'd never be forgiven if I didn't do the filial thing, obey the summons."

Eleanor suspects he's never rebelled at all. It's a pose. He needs his mother as much as she needs him.

Afterwards they walk back to her flat. It's not far. Nat doesn't drive. His flat overlooks the river, and he prefers public transport or taxis to the hassle of driving in the city.

"All those tourist hordes taking over again with the summer," he looks at a group of Americans with distaste. He'll spend his summer buried in the Rare Manuscripts room where only visiting scholars have access. He doesn't mind them.

His fingers are strong. Eleanor revels in being played like a piano. He's a generous lover. She will miss him.

"When are you coming back?" he asks as they sprawl with a drink afterwards.

"I'm probably not," she looks at him lazily. "Will you mind?"

"French shores more attractive, eh."

"Time I had a sabbatical."

"We might meet in Paris some time then," he's unfazed. His work takes him to other libraries in other cities often enough.

"That could be possible." She's conceding nothing. Nat is a London link, not a French one. He'll stay separate, and no longer part of her life. She gets up and puts on coffee. Time to ease him out. She has a dinner date later.

He watches her pad naked around the flat. His eyes are pensive, rather dejected for a moment, then he obviously thinks of something else, a book perhaps, as he pulls on his clothes again. Eleanor hands him coffee and puts on her robe, sitting on the small sofa by the window where she can see trees in the park opposite. There are tight small buds that will soon be leaves. It's spring. Time for a new departure.

Chapter Seven

Roz slams into the house and puts down her shopping. Nothing's right. Her kindergarten class in the morning all misbehaved, the supermarket hasn't got the tea she wants, and Bill, well, Bill is the real cause of her anger. There's Paula swanning off on some glamorous holiday in France and Bill wants to take her and their two boys on holiday in the Australian outback. Life is so unfair. And now she has to mop up the egg that broke when she crashed the shopping bags on to the bench. Curses. Multiple curses. Why isn't she going to France. It'll be wasted on Paula, she hasn't got an ounce of adventure in her, can't even dredge up any enthusiasm for a randy Welshman. What wouldn't Roz do with a chance to get away like that. Away from this whole boring life.

She picks up another egg and hurls it at the cupboard. Then another. It's only mildly satisfying and she still has to clean up the mess. Paula should be so smug. Gordon's a whole heap sexier than Bill, boring old solicitor.

To top it all off, she was out voted by the other two producers at the meeting about the play dates. So she has to get Gareth up to scratch before Easter. And Paula's won again. It's all such a pain. And no way is she going to holiday in the Australian outback. Bill can take the boys on his own. She will at least stay in Sydney and go shopping instead. That'll teach him.

Whoops. That's Paula's car in the drive. What possessed her to suggest reviving the old habit of having dinner together with the children on the men's Rotary nights? It faded when the children were older and needed ferrying in so many different directions after school. It's her own idea too, inviting Paula to dinner after work so they're not both eating on their own. Will there be enough eggs left for an omelette? Only Paula will expect more than that. Roz has a reputation to keep up after her Cordon Bleu cooking course on that one long ago overseas trip with Bill, while he went to some Oxford thing.

She grabs the cooking wine and takes a big swig just as the doorbell rings and the door opens. They always have free entry into each other's homes. Paula's her oldest friend here for goodness sake. They've shared all the pregnancies, small children, school committees and so on. She has to dredge up some pleasure in Paula's excitement about her trip, if only she doesn't go on about it tonight.

"I'm whacked. Such a luxury not to have to feed myself, thanks." Paula flops on to a kitchen stool, watching Roz wipe egg off cupboards with no sign of even noticing anything unusual.

"Have some wine," Roz pulls out a new bottle of red from the grocery bags, handing it to Paula with the opener. As Paula goes to work on it she puts the big pot on for pasta and finds the cream and vegetables for the sauce. Keep it simple. Just as well they're in the kitchen and she can concentrate on what she's doing while she calms down and smoothes her face.

Paula finds glasses and pours her a generous one.

"Signed a petition today," she says.

"Making the main street a mall, is it?"

"Not this time. The supermarket want that little park for a car park."

"I should think you would sign. How can I?"

"It'll be in the library for a few days."

"Bet your Miss Gray didn't sign."

"Of course she did. She's in favour of making the road a mall too."

"That surprises me."

"All that motor pollution dust is bad for books, it really accumulates."

"Yes, I bet you count all of five cars passing when you spend half an hour in the window!"

They both laugh. Roz is loosening up. Paula is good company. She'll miss her. How dare she be away so long.

"Hope you know your lines. The plays are in the week before Easter now."

"Oh good. You know I know them."

"Gareth'd better learn them quickly." Roz tips meat into the sizzling fry pan, stirs it for a while then puts the lid on. She pours more wine while they wait till it's time to put the pasta in. Then she washes the greens and whirls them in the salad drier.

When it's ready they carry plates, food and wine into the dining room. Roz and Bill live in the original old farm house near the top of the hill on the outskirts of town. Gordon built a new place in a dead end side street half way up the hill. The irony is that Roz would have loved a gleaming efficient new home, while Paula covets the style of old wooden floors and panelling and high ceilings.

"So why don't you have a fling with Gareth to warm you up for the French," Roz shoots off as they sit down.

"You can't be serious!"

"If you could see the two of you acting together, real sparks of fire. You should go for it."

"It's just the play. It comes alive."

"You come alive more like. Time you did."

"You're joking."

"Aren't you tempted?"

"It's not possible. Not here."

It's an admission Roz seizes on.

"So you're tempted but you're waiting till you get away."

"No no. Of course not."

"Don't you ever get bored with small town life?"

"I don't think that's the way to relieve boredom."

"Lucky you, off to France. No-one will ever know what you get up to over there." Roz speaks more emphatically than she intends.

"That's not what I'm going for."

"Be nice to have a bit of excitement."

"Oh Roz, are you that bored?"

"Yes. Our men are so beastly smug and contented with their tiny lives in a small town."

"Suppose they are a bit."

"I just want to break out sometimes, cause a scandal, shock everyone out of their complacency."

"Hey, slow down. You need watching. What are you planning in my absence?"

"Don't worry. It'll be you having all the excitement. We can't all be high on your trip all the time you know." She's revealing too much bitterness, time she shut up.

"You should talk Bill into letting you go somewhere interesting in the holidays."

Then it all spills out, Bill's suggestion, her anger, how much she doesn't want to go to the Australian outback. Paula is sympathetic. But of course it's easy for her, she won't be there. Roz allows her anger to show. Even telling Paula that Bill objects to her staying in Sydney because the friends they visit there include an old boyfriend of hers.

"He's so archaic, he doesn't trust me. I really miss not having another woman in the family. Why didn't I have a daughter like you?"

"You can borrow mine if you think it would help."

Roz looks at Paula in amazement. What an idea.

"Would she like a week in Sydney do you think?"

"Are you serious? She'd go spare at the thought."

Roz likes the proposal. She knows Emma won't make the demands on her she would on her mother, and she'll be good company shopping. What's more, Bill can't possibly object if she has a young teen to look after. They plot and plan as Roz's mood lifts. Goodbye the Australian outback. She can do what she likes in Sydney, her friends are bound not to mind babysitting a bit. All she has to do is check it out with Gordon and his mother, but Paula doesn't see any problem there.

Sydney may not be France but at least it's a whole world away from Rivertown.

Chapter Eight

Dear Nell,
This will be the last letter there's time for but I shall phone you again. Yes it did seem a bit daring to call you Nell again, I needed to be given permission. Don't you realise how awesome you are?
The play went really well. Full house on the last night. I'd say thousands turned away but it is just a small town with no spare thousands around. Anyway it was fun, and I got disgustingly high on both the performance and the party afterwards. Nearly disgraced myself with the dashing Welsh school teacher who played Smirnov. Yes, school teachers here can be interesting. We get a lot of the new international arrivals who do their time in a small town before moving on to bigger things. Makes the drama group a bit more inspiring anyway. Didn't think I needed that much frivolity though. Especially now it's nearly time I'm off. Just a work dinner for Gordon's staff and then the children at Easter, ten whole days of them, and I'm on my way.
Nora's been great. You may even be impressed with what she managed to find in Auckland shops. I was. A new hair cut too, but still li'l ol' me inside. We went to a 'modern' Shakespeare at the Watershed Theatre in an old warehouse near the wharves. Now I'll have something to compare with the London theatre. Roll it on!
The English spring sounds so good, hope it lasts till I get there.

See you soon!
YoP
Polly.

The staff dinner Thursday night is an anniversary celebration. It's ten years since the first branch opened. Now the staff of all five branches are coming to the catered dinner in the Masonic Hall. Roz and Bill will be there too. He's the firm's solicitor. Paula decides to wear her new dress, the burgundy one bought with Nora, who's coming with them and wants to see how it looks.

"You should go shopping more often," Gordon's approval is warm. He may not have noticed how the rich colour brings out the lights in her hair, but he certainly appreciates the overall effect.

"Lynne's coming?"

"Yes of course. They're probably already in town having a drink."

Lynne is Gordon's first woman manager. Paula likes her a lot. She's an unmarried career woman, capable and very efficient, with two business degrees and experience in a city manufacturing business. Paula was amazed that she wanted to leave the city, but it was to look after her elderly mother in the coastal town where Gordon was opening the third branch, five years ago. When Gordon brought the applications home to consider it was Paula who encouraged him to take a chance on a woman. He was conservatively doubtful as to how she would fit in with the predominantly male workforce. She was by far the best qualified. He appointed her, and has never had cause for regret. In fact Lynne's branch has the consistently best figures, and even though other managers say it's because her town is bigger, it's obvious that more happens in her branch than in the others.

Nora approves of Paula's appearance, and when they arrive Roz hails her with lavish praise.

"Your choice, Nora? Isn't she smashing in it?"

Gordon smiles with pride as she stands beside him to welcome everyone, chatting with them all, meeting new staff members for the first time, renewing old acquaintanceships. Gordon is in good form, surrounded by all his men, joking with them. She manages to sit next to Lynne at their table.

"So you're off shortly."

"Twelve days to go. I feel so fortunate, Gordon's letting me go off like this."

"Perhaps he's the fortunate one. You're leaving him free too, you know."

"Oh. I hadn't thought of that!"

"Just teasing. You don't need to worry with Gordon."

"That makes him sound a bit boring." Roz is opposite them.

"Not boring," Lynne is emphatic. "You haven't heard him on incentives at a staff meeting!"

"Wish I could," Roz is intrigued.

The food comes, followed by speeches and jokes before they can mingle and talk again, while the tables are cleared and the hired local dance band moves in.

"How's your mother?" Paula finds herself with Lynne again.

"Not so well actually. They've put her into hospital for tests."

"I am sorry."

"She's quite enjoying bossing them all around. And I must admit I'm finding it quite good to have a break. Even with the hospital day care callers it's getting a bit much for me to manage."

"It must be hard, working full time too."

"I need to get someone in for the evenings I'm out now. She had a nasty fall a while ago when I was at a film."

"It's a worry isn't it. We're lucky Nora's so fit, and my mother has already bought a cottage in a retirement village. She moved in a couple of months ago and she's loving it. Swimming, all the group activities. She's usually far too busy to come and visit us now!"

Gordon has the first dance with his mother. She's ready to go then, so Gordon slips out briefly to take her home.

Roz joins them. "Must feel a bit funny for Nora, seeing how big it's all grown."

"I think she enjoys not being involved now. Good to come to something like this, but since Joseph died she hasn't really wanted to know."

"Shows confidence in Gordon anyway."

"Oh yes. She's always had that."

Gordon returns and asks Lynne to dance. He's followed by Hoani, another manager, who takes Paula onto the floor. She loves his sense of rhythm and always enjoys dancing with him.

"Off on the big trip eh!"

"It all seems a long way from this."

"Don't worry. We'll still all be here when you get back."

"How are Moana and Sam?" Hoani is very proud of his small children, and happy to talk about them.

"We're having another one."

"Great. When?"

"September."

"I should be back by then."

"You're going for that long?"

"Well, two or three months anyway. I want to make it worth while since it's so far."

"Gordon's going to miss you," the simple statement of fact is so different from what her other friends have been saying.

"Yes. I'll miss him too."

"He works so hard. He needs a holiday too."

It's the first time anyone has made her feel even the slightest bit guilty about leaving Gordon. She knows it's just Hoani's way, that he can't conceive of a married couple travelling away from each other.

Hoani takes her back to sit with Mere for a while, getting them both orange juice. Paula is amused at his male assumption that, like his wife, she too will want orange juice. Mere also expresses surprise that she's off on her own, but she accepts it without hesitation.

"Good on you. Now your children are big. Clever of you to stop after two," and she laughs, touching her own expanding stomach.

"You'll be pleased though. Nice to have them not too far apart."

"Moana is already choosing names. Mostly ones she's given her dolls!"

"She'll love it. She would have been too small when you had Sam."

"Yes. Hoani wants another boy."

"Do you?"

"I don't mind."

"Suppose he wants a rugby team!"

"He won't be getting that, that's for sure!" and they both laugh. Hoani is a keen local player, coaching school boy rugby as well. He played for the province several times when he was younger and keenly follows the All Black and Shield matches. Paula has been to a number of games with Gordon and Simon. She's secretly relieved that Simon is not so keen and only plays in a minor team. She imagines most mothers would feel the same, considering how violent the game often seems to be. Then Gordon takes Mere onto the floor and she's caught up by Bill.

The first few dances are quite formal, only later breaking up into faster modern groupings, as ties come off, drinks loosen the more conservative, and the music heats up. Mindful of her unrestrained behaviour at the drama party last Saturday Paula is careful to only have the odd glass of wine and several juices. It would not do to let herself go here, where she is Gordon's wife before anything else. It's a pleasant knees up, not an abandoned rave. It even ends around midnight. Roz and Bill stay as they see off the last travellers, most of them having some way to go, although one group has booked into a local motel and will probably continue the party there.

"Kids tomorrow."

"Yours are on the early plane too?"

"Yes. See you there."

Paula takes off her new dress carefully, pleased with its success and wondering where she might be wearing it next. Gordon is satisfied with the evening. She mentions Lynne's mother, but he already knows, and says he told her to take time off if she needed it.

"She's too conscientious though. She doesn't need to ask my permission for time off, she's got good staff, she just won't take it."

"You're lucky aren't you? She must be one of the best."

"Good as a man any day," and that of course is the greatest praise he can give.

"You mean you won't be back for the May hols. I was going to ask Brian to stay."

"Perhaps this time you could go to Brian's."

"But..."

"He did come here in January."

The children are home and the house is full of noise and people, with dishes and clothes everywhere. Paula can hardly believe it's the same place. Were they always that rowdy, or has she just got so used to the peace without them?

"What are we going to do?" the questions are accusations.

"I'll be here. Granny will come when I'm at work." Gordon is calm, reassuring. He always has been. One word of his always has a magical effect on squally or squabbling children, while her words seem to bounce off them and be ignored, until she used to physically intervene, grab them apart, shout in a way she never intended to do, and kept vowing she would never do again.

"What will you bring back from Paris?" Emma eyes her doubtfully. Still ready to trade on her mother's freedom if it turns into something she wants.

"Malcolm's parents took them all to Europe last year. All four children, for two months." Simon is accusing, then speculative.

"No way." Gordon is definite. "Not with you two. You can save up and go yourselves, when you're old enough."

Who would want to travel with demanding teenagers, Paula thinks silently to herself, horrified at the idea of first seeing Europe that way. She loves her children dearly, but they have taken her over for so long. Now she knows what it's like to have a little time to herself.

The first day goes quickly, in the evening they all gather at their place for a barbecue. Bill and Gordon plan a fishing trip with the three boys, staying over night down the coast so they can go up one of the rivers.

"That leaves you and me and Emma. What will we do?"

"You could all come," Bill is magnanimous.

"No way. You only want a cook. We'll have our fun here."

"Sure you won't come Emma?"

"No. I don't want to get all wet and cold all the time."

"We don't want girls on this trip," her brother is scathing, but Emma has not the least desire to go. Even though she's going through a school girl crush on Michael, Roz's older son, she's sure a fishing trip would put her at a disadvantage with him. Paula and Roz are amused at how distance has suddenly lent enchantment to the rowdy childhood friendship.

The long weekend passes quickly. Paula and Roz take Emma to a craft fair in the country, where they see Hoani and Mere and their children. Paula buys little hand carved wooden boxes from Hoani's father, thinking they will make good gifts on her travels. Even Lynne has come through in search of bargains. On the way home they float the idea of going to Sydney to Emma. Predictably she's delighted, and can't wait to tell everyone. Her mother's going away is quickly overshadowed by the prospect of her own travels with Roz. When the men return Simon is quite jealous, until Bill suggests he join the trip to the outback. Paula doesn't care what they do. She can't wait to leave now, it's so close.

She escapes to the shop after Easter, while Emma is with Nora having fittings for a new dress. Emma has long scorned any attempt of Paula's to sew for her, and she's pleased that Nora offered, as she has a good eye and Emma has always loved the clothes she makes.

Miss Gray's friend is already coming in to help her through the lunch period, so Paula has arranged to take her out to a farewell lunch. Miss Gray has agreed, which is unusual in itself. Paula calls at Florence's shop and buys a big bouquet for her boss on the way. Miss Gray goes unusually pink with pleasure at the flowers, although she scolds her for the extravagance.

They go to the hotel, and Paula persuades her to indulge in a glass of wine as they eat their way through a three course lunch.

"I've brought a book for you," Miss Gray pulls a parcel from her bag. "You might like something to read on the plane."

Paula is touched and grateful. It's a thoughtful gesture. She opens it.

"The new Barbara Anderson. I wondered when it would arrive. Thank you so much."

"Your friend might be interested in a New Zealand writer too."

Miss Gray is being kind. Paula studies her while she eats. She could have been quite beautiful once, the cheek bones are good. She never wears any colour on her face, keeps her hair back so firmly. What was she like when she made that journey so long ago? Was her companion a man? A lover perhaps? If only she could find out. Miss Gray has given her the address of the London bookshop. She's hoping the owner will be able to help solve the mystery, if only she can work out how to ask about it.

"You'll like France," Miss Gray says unexpectedly.

"Did you spend much time there?"

"Quite a bit. Over several visits. The coast line can be very like New Zealand in places."

That's a novel thought. Paula doesn't want it to be too like home.

"Did you go there with your London friend?" she asks, daringly.

"Oh no. I used to visit her parents though, they spent a lot of time in the south. She was usually away at summer school."

"Do you think she'll like to meet me?"

"Yes of course. She's got a good mind, did well at Cambridge."

"Does she live right in London?"

"Yes. She has the old family apartment not far from Harrods, in an elegant old house on a square. Her mother only died a few years ago."

"Do you think she might like me to work in the bookshop for a while?"

"Not impossible. You'd like it, so many lovely old books she deals in. But you won't have time."

"It's just a thought."

"You mean as something to do if it doesn't work out with your friend?" Miss Gray's smile is both discerning and amused.

Paula grins back. "Don't suppose that will happen. It's just so long since I've seen her, and she's rather awesome."

"You can hold your own. Use that brain of yours, don't waste any chances while you're there."

It makes Paula feel guilty about what she's planning to use her brain to find out about Miss Gray. She orders coffee before Miss Gray has a chance to look at her watch. Her friend can cope a bit longer.

"Perhaps when you return I'll give you my little book to read, if you still want to."

That really makes her feel guilty.

"I'd love to see it."

"I wouldn't want you to get wrong ideas about Europe before you go. It's better to wait. To make your own impressions." This time Miss Gray does look at her watch, and starts gathering her bag and jacket.

"I'm seeing your mother-in-law tonight. She certainly works hard on the town improvement committee. We should be able to hold off that supermarket car park."

"I hope so."

"You won't need to worry about your family with Nora here, that must be a relief for you."

Paula can only agree. She walks Miss Gray back to the shop, giving her an awkward hug as she says goodbye.

"Look after yourself," her boss gives her a final thin lipped smile and turns into the shop. Paula walks back to her car. Then she drives to Nora's to pick up Emma. Everything seems to have the taste of being done for the last time. It shouldn't feel so final, surely, she's only going for a few months after all.

"This will be just right for Sydney," Emma twirls proudly, showing off her new dress. Her long hair, the same rich colouring as Gordon's, swirls out behind her.

"I expect your Auntie Roz will want to take you shopping," Nora says, putting away her sewing things. "I hope you'll lash out a bit in Europe too. Time you were extravagant about buying things for yourself." She looks at Paula.

Paula's surprised. Nora can still surprise her at times. She hasn't associated extravagance with Nora.

Gordon is becoming more and more like his father, she thinks that evening as he makes the last pronouncements to the children before they go back to school. They're leaving Sunday afternoon, and on Monday Gordon is driving her to Auckland to catch the plane. It's all happening too quickly now. She clings to Simon and Emma at the local airport, but they've already gone beyond her, mentally returned to the world of their school life. They won't even miss her in the holidays, so much will be happening for them. She feels a qualm of thwarted motherhood, but it's no use. They've grown past her, and she's going away herself. She doesn't want them to hold back, or so she assures herself.

As they drive out of town along the coast road on Monday she wonders when she'll see it again, how she'll feel. Gordon is quite silent on the journey. What is he thinking? Will he miss her? She tries to fill the spaces with chatter, but he has never liked chatter, he only answers in discouraging monosyllables.

They stop on the way for a tea break around Matamata. Paula leaves Gordon in the ruin of teacups and sandwich plates to go to the toilet. As she comes back into the café she is behind Gordon, and she sees he's talking quietly and urgently into his mobile phone. She assumes it's just another business call and comes up noisily beside him to sit down again. He looks up, startled, and hastily says goodbye to whoever it is, closing off the phone and putting it down.

"Time to go, then," he gets up.

It's not until later that she remembers his expression when he saw her. Odd. It didn't seem to fit with a business call at all. He talks a bit more on the last stage of the journey, almost as if he's the nervous one, not her. Or perhaps he's just trying to reassure her, he must have realised she wants to talk to pass the time so she can keep calm, not get too keyed up. He makes a joke of her nerves but he's abstracted all the same. It must be the unaccustomed volume of traffic as they approach the city, taking his attention on the motorway.

There's time for a last meal together before she has to check in. They stop at a hotel near the airport turnoff. It has a bar they've used before for meeting people.

"Will my bags be all right?" She watches him lock the car.

"Of course. Don't fuss. How will you manage travelling if you can't lose sight of your bags for five minutes?"

He's right, but she's still nervous. It's not the bags.

It's the whole thing. She wants reassurance. Gordon almost seems impatient to get away, to leave her on her own. Then he turns and smiles at her, gives her a quick hug as they walk in, and it's all right again. He does love her.

"Give yourself a decent feed," he hands her the menu in the restaurant. "Airline food is foul, you don't want to eat too much of it."

She lets him help her choose a huge meal, from shellfish to venison to a berry tart. She can't finish it all but it has calmed her down, eating, sipping the wine he chooses. It's as if she's already shaken off ordinary life and is on her way, Gordon with her for this part of the journey so it's safe. She doesn't want him to go. He seems to sense her reluctance and touches her more than he usually does, helping her with her coat, her bag, loading the trolley at the airport then taking the car to park it while she goes in to join the check in queue. He comes back to stand in line with her.

"Wish I was going now," he looks around the crowded airport, the air of expectancy such places generate, the flight calls hanging in the air, the mounds of luggage, the travellers anticipating hours in the unreal void of a plane then new destinations.

"I wish you were too," she clings to him.

"Maybe I'll join you somewhere on the way home."

"That would be great," she means it for the moment, but she can't imagine Gordon in Europe.

"You'll be right. Just hang on to your bag and watch out for strange men."

"Don't you trust me?" it's an attempt to be coy.

"Would you be going if I didn't?"

"I'm trusting you on your own too."

"With my mother to keep an eye on me? That's not trusting."

"You'll be OK?" her last desperate plea at the gate as he hugs her goodbye, then she's through and there's only time for a final wave before he's out of sight. The solid warm man who's been her security for so long.

It's like leaping off a cliff to travel without him. Then she scolds herself. This is her adventure. She doesn't need Gordon for it. She's on her way.

Chapter Nine

Eleanor looks around her flat critically. How will Paula see it? The second bedroom is very small, but it has a disproportionately large hand basin and room for a little table and chair by the window. If she fills it with flowers it should be all right.

Her job finished yesterday, she's free now, and off to meet friends in Hampstead for the day on the heath to celebrate. And to say farewell. She wants to get away soon after Paula's arrival on Tuesday, but supposes she'll have to give her time for a look at London, a bit of England. Her first visit so she'll want to see everything. How tedious. Eleanor hopes she'll be confident enough to sight see on her own, she's not going to spend all her time doing tours of the tourist spots. It's hard to imagine what Paula may have become if she hadn't opted for marriage and children in a small town. She laughs aloud thinking of that last letter. 'Nearly disgraced herself'. Typical Polly. Tempted but not falling. Maybe she'll change that away from home.

She decides not to take her car. It's easier in the underground and she's bound to be able to hitch a ride back with someone if she wants to. They're meeting at the Spanish Inn, so she'll take a cab there from the station. They'll be doing enough walking later. It's an unusually warm day for the time of year, still and sunny. When she arrives there's a group of people gathering outside the station for a guided walk around Hampstead. She must remember to see what's on for Paula in the way of walks, it's a great way to see a place, on foot with a commentary. Pity Paula's French may not be equal to doing the same in Paris.

Just as she looks for a cab a horn toots. It's a couple

on their way to meet her at the Inn so she joins them for the ride.

"We've been getting some goodies, there's a great deli here," Mandy turns to tell her. There's a huge wicker hamper in the back of the station wagon. They won't be walking far with that before they have lunch.

Eleanor's contribution is a bottle of wine in her shoulder bag and a gourmet pack of her favourite nuts. The wine is an award winning New Zealand sauvignon blanc, it's not half bad and she's found a good source near her flat. Paula might be impressed, although she'll probably prefer to try something more foreign. She makes a play of her origins whenever she produces a bottle and the only person who hasn't enjoyed it is Martin. So much for him, she grins to herself, remembering.

There are others already in the upstairs room of the Spanish Inn where they settle with a drink. They're all familiar with the dark heavy wooden tables and ancient beams, the atmosphere they take for granted. Eleanor looks around. There's not going to be much serious walking today, unless some of the males just peel off to stay in the bar, which they may well do. She suddenly feels hemmed in, wanting to get out in the open air, stride along the paths and through the trees.

"I'm going walking before lunch," she stands up, creating a moment of decision.

Several decide to join her, and they arrange a place to meet for the picnic later. Mandy thinks James, her husband, will manage to get the hamper along to a little grove they know, and she makes him set the alarm on his watch to remind him when to leave.

Eleanor is pleased to get outside. There are a number of walkers already on the heath. The bare trees are beginning to come to life again, there's even a glimpse of blossom up by the road. They turn away from it, seeking less trodden paths, as she strides ahead. Mandy keeps up with her, the others form groups trailing behind. Mandy's another hard worker in an international company. She's married, but has chosen not to have children, leading quite an independent life at times. She seems to think it's still worth being married, although Eleanor wonders. They worked together some years before, and have kept in touch. Mandy has a privileged background but she is socially unpretentious, which is why Eleanor likes her. Mandy prefers the natural look to the sophisticated shine of so many of her friends. Her long blonde hair is tied back with a scarf and her casual clothes do not have designer labels.

"So tell me about your friend. Shall we dine together one night?"

Eleanor finds herself talking about the past, the days studying with Paula in long ago Auckland. Only a few points of comparison with Mandy's Cambridge degree.

"So she's a bit of a follower. What do you plan to initiate for her on this trip?" Mandy is perceptive.

"A bit of excitement I suppose. I don't imagine she's had much adventure in a small town."

"How much adventure can she cope with?"

"We'll have to find out," Eleanor grins at her London friend. She'll have fun discussing Paula's summer with Mandy, who is so different from Paula. Then she remembers she's not expecting to return to London and she falls silent. Mandy and James are taking their holidays in the West Indies, sailing for most of it. She would have suggested they come to France, but there's no chance of that during the summer.

The air is clear on the hills of the heath, the branches still sharp etched against the blue sky, some buds not yet sprung. In summer it will not be so clear. Eleanor prefers it on days like this, cool enough to feel pleasure in walking a reasonable distance. Mandy asks about her plans after the summer and Eleanor is cagey, avoiding committing herself to a return. She lets Mandy think she's lining up work in France again. She probably will, it's a good idea. No need to think about it now though.

They're a long way from the meeting place when they

remember lunch, and everyone else has started by the time they return. They sprawl on rugs in the sun, passing food and wine, letting the afternoon laze away, out of the city, the pollution, the responsibilities of high powered jobs. It's an agreeable lazy day, and when Mandy and James drop her off later, turning down another drink because they're on their way to his mother's for dinner, Eleanor is pleased to be on her own. She's beginning to wonder what she's taken on for the summer. But Paula can't be too different, people don't change basically. She doesn't think they do.

On Monday she cleans the flat and buys fresh flowers. She puts a basket of English garden toiletries by the hand basin in Paula's room. One of her large soft teddy bears sits among the cheerful checked cushions on the bed. The matching curtains move in the slight breeze from the park. She sets the alarm in the evening to give herself plenty of time for the early flight arrival.

In the early hours she showers and dresses in her roomy bedroom, checking herself in the mirror. Lucky Paula had that naturally olive skin that tanned so easily, and has no doubt aged much better than hers. Will unobservant Paula notice the lines behind the careful makeup, the air of confidence? Eleanor is cynical about the chances of her doing so. She never did in the past. Eleanor knows how she looks because she's the one with merciless eyes, who is well aware of how much appearance can depend on art, indistinguishable from reality.

She sets off, skilfully negotiating the early morning city traffic, a reasonable run to reach the parking building near the terminal. She has mentally planned a route back into the city that will show Paula London at its best. She wants to shock Paula into realising that life is elsewhere and that she has been missing it in her small town.

There's a crowd waiting near the gate. Eleanor stands back a bit so she can see Paula coming without being part of the thrusting. Some passengers are already emerging. Is that Paula? No, too tall. She almost misses her as she comes through behind a family party, father wheeling a trolley overflowing with cases and soft bags and the toddler hanging on while his wife carries another infant. There's a moment as Paula stands, looking around expectantly, poised ready, while Eleanor examines her. Still slim in spite of two children. Hair still brown, straight and quite long, below a rather smart black felt hat. She's wearing pants and shirt for travelling, a sweater loosely knotted around her shoulders and a trench coat slung over the cabin bag and case on her trolley. Good skin, as she thought, tanned by the summer she's just left. Not much changed at all.

Then the moment passes, Paula sees her and Eleanor raises her arms in greeting.

Chapter Ten

After her second meal and film on the long flight Paula remembers the phone incident on the drive to Auckland. Once it comes back to her she can't get it out of her mind. It seems to add up to a number of other incidents. Gordon's moments of seeming to want to be rid of her, his offhand attitude to her travel plans, his cracks about her freedom on holiday. Then she reminds herself that he isn't free at all in his home town. It's silly to even think of other possibilities. He'd even been the one to suggest he might meet her somewhere on the way home. She starts watching another film and tries to forget about it, but the image of his face when he saw her starts to haunt her thoughts of him.

Later she forgets everything in the excitement of finally approaching London. Beneath the wings of the plane the misty patchwork fields of Kent unfold, there are glimpses of the city skyline in the distance. She's nervous in customs, sure they'll search her luggage, holding on firmly to her loaded shoulder bag, her one tightly packed case. The only delay is the long queue for foreigners, while all the languages of Africa and the European Common Market go straight through the English barrier. So much for ex colonials. Reality is Europe.

She's through. Will she recognise Eleanor? Is that her? She's standing slightly behind the crush of people waiting, she never was one for crushes. The hair is as blonde as ever, sleekly cut in a modern style that emphasises the natural wave and thickness. She's wearing black leggings and boots, with a bright red bulky jersey. Her arms rise in dramatic greeting and a smile breaks. Paula rushes into the warm embrace.

"You're looking good," Eleanor stands back at arm's length to look at her.

"You haven't changed at all!" Paula's eyes are blinded with delight.

"Tedious flight?"

"Not bad, had a shower in Singapore."

"It's horribly early. Nobody's got me up at this hour for yonks."

"Sorry."

"Don't apologise. Worth it. But I'm dying for coffee. Let's go."

Paula's bag is seized beyond protest and Eleanor leads her on a complicated route to the car park. Her senses are buzzing, she can't take it all in. She's really here, now, in London, with Eleanor. It's unreal. Eleanor has firmly rejected the airport coffee places and they zoom along the road into the city. Paula's head swivels, her eyes dart about trying to see everything at once. This is London. These row houses, the shabby industrial buildings as they leave the airport, they're totally different from home, they must be, she's travelled halfway around the world.

London is grey, grubby, uninspiring. Until they reach the city itself and Eleanor drives along beside one of the big parks. Suddenly it's all alive, the sun is coming through on the spring flowerbeds of tulips and vibrant colours, the bare branches have buds of leaves on them, some are even out. Now there's colour and excitement and Paula is waking up again with the new day. Eleanor casually points out buildings she's seen in books, on the screen. A palace, a monument, a cathedral. They're not real, it's like being part of a newsreel. Kensington and Green Park, Buckingham Palace, St James and Westminster. She doesn't ask herself if this is Eleanor's usual route or whether it's a deliberate attack on her senses. She's too blown away by it all. Eleanor has a little smile on her face, glancing at her from time to time as she drives expertly through the crowded streets with very little delay.

She doesn't even think about the miracle of Eleanor's easing into a parking space by another small park in a square. Here the sun has brought out a brushing of new green leaves above the iron palings. She can't take her eyes off the elegant old stone buildings around the square, all her preconceptions of London coming alive in front of her.

Eleanor leads her into a café in a small side street. They sit inside the window, the big glass doors opening at each new entry, the crowd at the bar counter deepening. The noise and steam of the espresso machine, the milk frothing, the cups clattering, and the level of talk, all make her head spin. The bite of strong coffee alerts her again, and there's a plate of fresh croissants on the table.

"Nothing at my place, and the croissants here aren't half bad." Eleanor puts sugar in her black coffee.

Paula stirs her cappuccino, takes a soft croissant. "They're great. Nothing like this at home, except maybe in the cities," she's a little defensive.

"You just wait," Eleanor is not going to let her stay defensive of home territory.

"Don't you eat at home?"

"Not much. I always was a lousy cook."

"Isn't eating out expensive?"

"Not necessarily. Saves time."

"Not sure whether I'm sleepy or just numbed."

"You need five hours fresh air and sunlight to adjust without jetlag. It's only seven thirty. Have another coffee."

Paula feels herself getting a second wind. People are filling the pavements and the shutters on shops are going up. It's chilly and still. She's been too stunned to talk much.

"Now I'll take you home for a shower and change, then we'll go out," Eleanor puts on her coat and gloves again, Paula follows.

It's only a short drive this time to Eleanor's quite spacious apartment in an old building with an ancient and unreliable lift. She's on the third floor. Paula is awed by the feeling of solidity and confidence in the quiet square. She stands at the tall windows overlooking the park with its iron railings, more spring green new leaves, bright flowers in the formal beds. There are colourful geraniums in the window boxes. Eleanor is smug about them.

"No use my planting bulbs, they'd die of neglect."

She puts Paula's case in the guest room. Paula picks up the huge bear and cuddles him, thinking of Emma's soft toys.

"In case you miss Gordon," Eleanor says airily. "My Aloysius is more huggable than lots of men. Most men."

"Is this really Bloomsbury?" Paula is still awed.

"Oh yes. Fringe. Not Russell Square."

"I can't take it all in yet."

"Plenty of time," they're back in the living room, Paula with her sponge bag and the large soft towel.

"And it's all yours," Paula looks at the sparse furniture, the well chosen pictures, the flashes of colour against the neutral background. It's totally Eleanor, stylishly casual, with an air of having just temporarily poised in one place. She finds it hard to imagine living like this, no garden, no space to separate it from the neighbours. Eleanor is obviously amused at the artless remark.

"I'm subletting it for the summer. Some Americans who actually want to spend a summer based in London. They can have it."

How can Eleanor be so casual about living in London, Paula thinks as she goes to shower. It's all inconceivable, her friend's life. She hears Eleanor in the kitchen, a kettle boiling, as she dresses after the shower. She hangs the clothes from the top of her case in the tiny closet, puts her makeup on the small chest with its spring flowers, lavender sprays. Eleanor offers her a choice of juices or herb teas when she emerges, a skirt not too crumpled, her shirt fresh.

They sit at the table in a window with fragrant mugs

of minted tea. Paula has been into the compact kitchen now, seen the full extent of Eleanor's space.

"Don't you miss... I mean, wouldn't you like to have had a family, a permanent home?" It's too early for such questions but Paula can't help herself. Eleanor knows she was never renowned for tact. She looks at Paula, amused again.

"What's it like, having children, the maternity bit?" She speaks as if the thought is a foreign country.

"I wouldn't have missed it. Haven't you, ever?"

"Missed it? Well, it's a bit late for that now."

"You mean you might have, once?"

"I only thought about it."

"No regrets?"

"Sometimes I think... you know... there'll be nothing left of me." Eleanor avoids her eyes a moment to look out the window.

"Oh Nell. Wasn't there ever anyone?"

Eleanor laughs. "If you think I need a man for it. Yes. Not usually available though."

Paula finds it too difficult to put herself in Eleanor's place. The idea of such a life, so many changes, is alien to her. The security of Gordon has been too important.

"There're lots of single mothers now."

Eleanor looks surprised. "I couldn't now even if I wanted to."

"Why not?"

"An abortion too many." She notices Paula's face. "Polly, you silly fool, what did you think I did?"

"I suppose I didn't think."

"Such a lovely insulated life you lead with Gordon. I did envy you at times."

"You envy me?" Paula is amazed. Another alien concept while her mind is still scrambling to cope.

"Why not?"

"Your life is so full, exciting. I never thought..."

"No, I guess not. Neither do I much. Only occasionally when things aren't going well. Then there's a new and exciting job, place or man, and I forget again."

"There must be plenty left."

"It can't go on forever."

"You look so good still."

"There's no going back," Eleanor's philosophical, although she enjoys her friend's appreciation.

"Do you still not want to settle anywhere?" Paula is curious.

"Certainly not with a Gordon in New Zealand, if that's what you're thinking. Possibly somewhere, with the right person."

"Have you ever lived with anyone?"

"Several times. Only ever worked for a few months. Wrong chaps though."

"Why?"

"Perhaps we didn't have enough in common after all."

"But I think it's better if you're not too much alike."

"Well, it worked for you," but Eleanor suspects that years of marriage, especially to Gordons, make people more alike. She refrains from saying so.

"We seem to balance well," Paula is thoughtful, even wondering how well they do balance.

"Maybe I need an opposite, someone complementary," Eleanor is enjoying the game of speculation now.

"Can't quite see you."

"Nor can I. You can keep your opposite, if he is."

"If I want to," the words slip out, thoughtless.

Eleanor stares at her. "Oh no, Polly. Not you."

"I didn't mean, well, I don't know, it just came out. I hadn't thought."

"Oh dear. Don't let it be me who makes you question your life. I only offer a break from it."

"Maybe I need that break more than I realised."

They stare at each other, eyes suddenly naked. There's too much truth in the room and Eleanor wants to stop before it goes too far.

"Come on. Aren't you ready yet?" She holds out

Paula's coat. "Lots of walking before lunch."

"Just have to put some makeup on." Paula goes back to her room.

She's back in the living room before Eleanor returns from getting her coat. Paula is looking at the loaded bookshelves, touching one of a scatter of paperweights.

"You can read later. I'll let you have a siesta this afternoon."

"Sorry, I didn't want to..."

"Please stop apologising. I can't stand apologies."

Paula bites her lip as she's swept off. No car this time, they're exploring on foot, down through the theatre district to Covent garden. Paula is fascinated by the market stalls, the bustle and life of so many people, all in such a hurry, except the buskers and the beggars by the ancient church theatre. Eleanor's told her the only way to explore London is on foot. She's trying to resist buying too many things at once, but her bag is bulging with knick knacks by the time Eleanor leads her out of the small alleys and into a central courtyard filled with café tables. Paula's amazed to realise the morning has gone, it's nearly lunch time.

"Can't do too much at once," Eleanor chooses a table, looks at a menu. The café is already nearly full. "Bit of a tourist trap this, but still, a lot of locals wander around."

Paula is watching everything avidly, storing images, thinking how she'll never be able to describe it all, but at the same time deciding on the words she'll use to write to the children, to Roz. She can hardly eat the plate of salad that comes, though it's nice to sit down. She's not used to the constant noise, the level of action all around her. Eleanor doesn't seem to notice it but it's an assault on her senses, already reeling from the flight.

She's grateful when they leave the market, going down the narrow streets to the Thames.

"Just a walk by the river and we'll get the underground back," Eleanor says.

This is the Thames, Paula tells herself, that was

Covent garden. I'm really here.

They walk along the embankment, through narrow parks and past statues among green bushes.

"Don't think I can take in much more," Paula says, as they sit on a winged wrought iron bench, watching the river traffic.

Eleanor looks out over the river, its murky waters flowing swiftly, the river boats and tugs and curls of smoke.

"So what do you want to do in London?" she asks.

"Well," Paula doesn't know where to start. Then she remembers. "I've got the address of a woman with an antique bookshop I'd like to visit."

"You mean you know someone?"

"It's this friend of Miss Gray's, the lady I work for."

"Can't get away from it huh!"

"There's a bit of a mystery I want to solve, actually."

"Detective work in London," Eleanor sounds cynical.

Paula launches into the story of Miss Gray's travels and her mystery companion, telling her about finding the travel book. Eleanor grins. This is a new side to Paula, on the trail of someone's past. The old Paula wouldn't have been so decisive in pursuit. Eleanor looks at the address Paula pulls out of her bag.

"Do you want me to come with you?"

"If you like.'

"No. Better if I just drop you off."

They decide to leave it for another day. Paula is feeling rather dazed, and fortunately it's not far to the nearest underground station. She remembers the fire of several years before as they go down the long escalators, but Eleanor tells her it's all been cleaned up since, and certainly it seems clean and busy. The press of people is almost too much, but Eleanor guides her through, up and down stairs and along tunnels like an automaton until they're on a platform and there's a rush of air and noise and dust as a train roars out of the darkness and pulls up beside them. The rest is a blur of trying to keep her feet in the crowded train, being pushed along more tunnels and stairs and into a huge lift that fills with people before rising up to let them out on to the street near Russell Square.

She's allowed a sleep before dinner. Then Eleanor takes her to a small cheerful Italian restaurant nearby, no major effort needed, green checked cloths and tasty pasta, a short walk home and she really flakes this time.

In the next few days Paula is swept away into a blur of images and new experiences. It's neither difficult nor strenuous. Eleanor's version of sight seeing is to drive past most of the tourist sights, pointing them out dismissively and saying she can return for a proper look later if she likes. She does walk through her personal favourites with Paula though, Westminster Abbey and St Pauls, several London parks with flower beds and water and children playing, all with frequent pauses to sit and look, to take a drink, a leisurely lunch.

Then for about a week they drive around Cambridge, Oxford, the Cotswolds, a little of South England and Wales, stopping at small pubs or bed and breakfast places that charm Paula. They see live Shakespeare in Stratford, listen to jazz outdoors at a country mansion, walk through the gardens of stately homes and castles. Nothing is rushed, that isn't Eleanor's style. She watches Paula, assessing each impression made on her and keeping it whole. All the time they talk, and the years fall away.

At first they talk about the past, reliving student days, laughing and sharing memories. Then they start spanning the years, Paula spilling out the details of life in a small town, life with Gordon, Roz, the children. Eleanor even seems interested, keeps her talking with questions. She's not so forth coming about the details of her own life, dismissing the years with scanty reference to various jobs, places, people. Then she seems to relent and starts outlining several of her relationships, imitating the men and sending up their more conventional attitudes so that Paula falls about laughing and feels as if they're back in student days again. Eleanor the mimic, who could always make her laugh. Laughter spans the years and bridges any gaps in their friendship.

Then they're back in London. Eleanor wants to leave in a couple of days, but she needs to do several things first. Paula is free to wander the city again, exploring galleries and famous shopping streets. In the evenings they go to a show, dine with several of Eleanor's London friends, have drinks with another group, go on to a club. If Eleanor has been aiming to turn her head she succeeds.

At last Paula has time to find the antique bookshop belonging to Miss Gray's friend. It's near the British Museum, in one of the busy side streets with several other book shops. She walks there, checking the map first. Eleanor has arranged to meet her for lunch in a wine bar near by, pointing it out on the map.

Cholmondeley Books has a narrow street frontage when Paula identifies it, having walked right past it once. There is only one window, where several antique books are displayed against a grey draped background. Paula notices that one is French, an early edition of a Balzac novel.

She pushes the heavy door with its small open sign and notices of literary meetings on the inside of its upper glass panel. A discreet bell tinkles her arrival. She draws an audible breath on the threshold, breathing in the smell of books, not musty but heady, that of well loved and looked after old books, filling the floor to ceiling shelves of the narrow space that reaches back into dim recesses behind a big oak table three quarters of the way down. Comfortable chairs are scattered for browsers, and wooden steps for reaching the upper shelves. The wooden staircase at the back goes up to a mezzanine floor, where glass cases protect the rarest books.

A grey haired man with a domed forehead and rimless glasses is sitting in one of the chairs, a large volume open on the reading lectern beside him. He turns a page carefully.

Paula takes another deep breath and walks past him towards the big table. Behind it a woman is sitting at a small desk against the side wall. For a moment it reminds her of Miss Gray, sitting over her accounts, then the woman looks up, and although the stance is the same she can see that this woman is much younger, near her own age.

"I'm Paula," she holds out her hand. "I think Miss Gray wrote to you."

"Oh yes," the voice is warm and friendly, the hand clasp firm and brief. "Call me Antonia."

Antonia's hair is swept back in coils either side of her face, giving her a slightly old fashioned look. It's glossy brown, and her eyes glow brown too behind the burgundy framed glasses. Paula follows her neat figure in its tailored skirt and silk blouse through to a tiny back room, where Antonia puts on her electric jug and clears an antique tapestry chair for Paula to sit on. The room is crammed with more books, papers, aged and worn chairs and small tables, with a little sink and shelf in the corner where Antonia takes up delicate bone china to put on a round table near Paula. There is a glint of amusement in her eyes as she watches Paula taking everything in.

"Tell me about Virginia, about her shop. I want to know the real details please, she doesn't tell me enough when she writes."

Paula does her best, balancing fine china, trying not to knock anything over with her knees, her elbows. At last Antonia's avid questions seem to be satisfied.

"Do you know about her travel book?" Paula asks tentatively.

"Yes. It was my father who took it to a publisher."

"I was hoping you might have a copy of it I could buy." Paula hardly dares ask.

"I think the last one went long ago, but I'll have a look. I've one at home if you haven't read it."

"Did you see a lot of her when she was here?"

"She met my parents in the south of France one year. She was writing up her travel journal and showed it to them. My father thought it was very good and persuaded her to let him show it to a publisher he knew."

"What was she like then?"

"She was very reserved, but my parents really liked her. They spent a lot of time together in France over several years. My parents usually went south there in winter. She was a good friend, even helping out in the shop when my mother was ill once."

"So you knew her well."

"Not me so much. I was studying then, or travelling around Europe with my friends. We'd only stay there a few days. I liked Virginia's painting though, very talented. Did she keep it up?"

"Painting? I didn't know she painted." Paula's amazement is loud in the small room.

"She was good. She mostly painted in Brittany though, near the south coast where Gauguin used to go. How sad that she stopped."

They are silent for a moment, then Paula's questions start, and Antonia tells her about the places Miss Gray went in France. She recognises the name in Brittany, she must have seen it on the map near where she's going with Eleanor.

Paula is thrilled. So much more information, and mystery, but there is no more to learn here. They talk books again, and Antonia shows her around the shop, pulling treasures out of the glass cases or climbing the steps to fetch something else down. Then Paula stands looking at the volumes she's collected on the oak table while Antonia searches the shelves right at the back. There is a little sound of triumph as she pulls out the small black book with its photo of Lake Baikal.

"Here you are. Must be the last one. I'd overlooked it."

Paula is effusive in her delight. She pulls out her

purse, but Antonia refuses payment.

"It's my gift to you. It's been such a pleasure to talk about Virginia and my parents. Please remember I'd love to know what happened about her painting. My parents had several, but I'm not sure where they are. I'll have to ask my brother, he has their house in the country."

It is time to meet Eleanor, and the bell from the book shop door has sounded several times as people enter. They clasp hands warmly, and Paula leaves with a light step, bubbling and excited as she goes to the rendezvous.

The wine bar is obviously familiar to Eleanor. They sit outside by a big planter in the courtyard, where sun is finding the stones and sparrows are chasing crumbs. Eleanor listens to Paula's description of Antonia and the shop, all she has found out, and the special bonus of Miss Gray's book, which Paula gives her to look at.

"So where is this place in Brittany?" she asks at the end of Paula's recital.

"It's Pont Aven. Is that how you say it?"

"No. Bretons often accent the last syllable in a very unFrench way. It's Pont Av_en_, and that's the famous artists' village where Gauguin painted and every budding artist has set up an easel and a gallery ever since."

"Is it really close?"

"About ten minutes. Everything's close there."

"I'd love to go there. See if there's any trace of her."

"Goodness knows where you'd start. I think you're dreaming."

"I'd like to try anyway."

Paula is obviously determined and excited by her discovery. Eleanor looks at her coolly. She dabbled in painting, in the south of France, herself. She's not going to admit to it yet, although one of her water colours hangs in Paula's room. It's of the Tour Fenestrelle in Uzès, and it rather pleases her. Unsigned of course. She's planning to time her disclosures to Paula. Not too many shocks at once.

Eleanor decides to take her own car to France, rather than sell it and buy or hire another as she originally intended.

"Must be getting old. I prefer the familiar," she remarks as they load it to leave for the ferry. They stop for a meal near Dover before the car ferry leaves, gazing out over the sea. Eleanor is pensive.

"Dover Beach. Shades of time past."

"Such a haunting poem. I tried to repeat its rhythm once. Didn't work for me of course."

"You still write poetry Polly?"

"At times. Only if it comes."

"You should have kept it up. You were good."

"Too much else to do. Don't you still?"

"My doggerel? You must be joking."

Paula looks at her friend, the planes of her face, the cheek bones, the fine skin which is English pale. She feels a rush of warmth, of love. She's not going to let Eleanor disappear again from her life.

Dear Roz,
Well it's all been great. So much happening there's hardly been time to write until now on the ferry. We've been whizzing around London and most of South England. Found Miss Gray's friend in London. Delightful lady, only about our age. She made me tea in this tiny back room crammed with antique furniture and books, using a huge silver teapot with old bone china teacups. I was scared to move in case I dropped something.
She gave me several books for Miss Gray that I've already posted. Wish I could have kept them, but I did indulge in a lovely old edition of Elizabeth Barrett Browning's poems. It's so hard to resist all the latest books and in fact I haven't. They come out in paperbacks so much

more quickly than at home. I'll post them for you to read when I've finished. I've sent the children some books too.

Everything is wonderful. Eleanor is so glamorous and I admire her tremendously. Super apartment, knows everyone and everything. Guess we're both still much the same underneath, still talking all the time. Perhaps time will slow down a little once we settle in France.

Hope all's going well there. Do tell me all about the next play and what else is happening. Gordon only sends brief notes that don't say much, or rings and sounds quite preoccupied on the phone. Give my love to everyone, well I mean selectively!

Love,
Paula.

Chapter Eleven

They make their leisurely way across Normandy, detouring to Bayeux and then to Rheims and the champagne district. Finally they move into a small but elegant apartment in the Passy quarter of Paris. Eleanor announces offhandedly that it belongs to a friend currently working in Tahiti, and they're just lucky enough to get it for a week between tenants. She notices that Paula has ceased to show amazement at her network of friends and connections. She watches Paula soak up Paris as if she has been waiting all her life for just this moment.

"It's not that anything surprises me. I already knew it so well, it feels familiar, just as England did."

"It's a home coming of sorts."

"That's exactly it."

"Are you understanding more in the cafés?" They're sitting outside one in the Latin Quarter, after visiting the Cluny, and several churches in the area. In spite of the greater expense of sitting outside, Paula cannot resist the pavement tables. Eleanor feels indulgent as her friend soaks up the atmosphere that has become part of her own life. She doesn't normally stand at the zinc herself, although while it's still inclined to be cool she would probably be sitting inside. They keep their jackets on. Already in May Paris is filling with tourists.

Paula is stroking the marble of the little round table with her fingers, brushing the tiny dish with the bill in it. Their bentwood chairs are in a row facing the street behind the double line of tables. Paula can't get over the fact that they all face out, no sign of a conversational grouping. The better to see and be seen, Eleanor assures her.

"It's still rather like music washing over me, but I'm getting a bit more."

"It'll come. We should speak French more. Didn't you say you'd been talking French in your head at home?"

"Yes, but it's a bit different when you get an answer!"

Eleanor looks speculatively at Paula. She's hoping her friend will prove amenable to whatever might happen in the summer. She has not yet told her about possibilities that may change the original plans. Paula's so happy with everything she suspects she'll get away with just about anything.

She takes Paula to wander in the spring gardens, the galleries, the markets, and along the bouquinistes by the Seine. Often she sees someone she knows, and they stop at the nearest café for a drink and a rapid French conversation. Paula sits bemused and smiling. Eleanor tries to include her, or else the friends try their English on her.

"Tell me about New Zealand." Eleanor grins to herself as Michel, a Parisian jeweller, sits very close to Paula, repeating in a lyrical English accent the same words he used on her when they were introduced years before. His tight jeans and loose black shirt, open nearly as far as the waist, are almost a uniform among his friends, as is the designer stubble on his lean jaw. He stays seated because he is quite short. Paula is opening up under his expert attention, talking enthusiastically. Her other friend, Marc, watches closely too.

"Et toi. Viens," he takes her hand urgently.

She looks at Paula, assessing how long her conversation might continue. Then her own urges take over. "Got something to do. Mind if I go off for a while?"

Paula looks both startled and confused.

"Won't be long. Meet you back here in about an hour." She doesn't wait for a response, just walks off with Marc. When she glances back from the corner Paula is still looking at her, while Michel signals the waiter for another drink.

"You cannot live in each other's pockets. Michel will

look after her," Marc puts his arm around her and his graceful stride matches hers. They are the same height. His legs are longer than Michel's, his jeans more battered. There is a careful quiff of hair falling over his high forehead, almost to his large nose, of which he is proud because of its alleged sexual implication. His apartment is only two blocks away. Eleanor puts any guilty thought right out of her mind. Paula's not a child, and it's a long time since she's had a chance to indulge herself with Marc. He's such uncomplicated good company, no strings and no complexes, just a healthy physical relationship.

When they return to the street close to an hour later, she feels so good she thinks it might be dangerous to go back to Paula until the glow wears off.

"I need an apéritif right now," she says, pulling Marc into his corner bar. He hasn't thought to provide anything. Typically he never eats at home.

"So why are you vanishing into Brittany?"

"I need a holiday."

"Let your friend go. Have a holiday here with me."

"Too much going on here. I'd never relax."

"I relax you," no false modesty either.

"You can visit us if you like."

"Me in Brittany? You joke."

"You could do with some air," she teases him, knowing it would take more than herself to prise him from his beloved Paris.

"I would miss too much here. You know the season is coming to a peak. Why don't you stay?"

"I don't want to. Not this time." She's as direct as he is. They grin at each other in mutual appreciation.

"Another?"

"No. We must move. We can have one back there."

Paula looks as if she hasn't moved in their absence. Michel is still talking eloquently, waving his hands close to her face, touching her arm. She looks up gratefully at Eleanor's return. Michel stops talking long enough to run his eyes frankly over both of them and wink discreetly, while he shrugs with a gesture towards Paula that she cannot see.

"She has not convinced me that I need to visit New Zealand," he tells the others.

"Of course not. What could the end of the world have to offer after Paris?" Marc is even more dismissive. Eleanor sits down quickly to avoid his hand running any further down her back.

"You've only got one evening left to convince Paula of anything. We're leaving tomorrow."

"So soon?"

"We're going to the sea. Paris can't offer that," Paula obviously still thinks she might convince them Paris doesn't have everything, but Eleanor knows it's a lost cause.

"Rue Jacob tonight?" Marc looks at her insistently.

"Maybe. Got to have an early night though if I'm driving."

"What's in Rue Jacob?" Paula's eyes follow them.

"Just a jazz club. We'll have to eat first." Eleanor hopes the men will leave. She's languid and satiated and she can see Paula is ready to return to the apartment.

"We'll see you later. Want to meet for dinner?" Marc won't let her off so easily.

"I don't think so. We might bump into you somewhere," she stands, her coffee finished. "Come on Polly."

Paula starts questioning her about the men as they walk down to the metro.

"You didn't like Michel much then?" Eleanor tries to put her off.

"Oh he's all right. What do you mean?"

"Nothing. Let's have a rest before we go out again," she closes her eyes on the train to discourage talking. Her mind goes dreamily over the last hour or so. She decides Paula will just have to be as tolerant as she unwittingly was in her innocent student days.

"We're nearly there," Paula nudges her.

"Plenty of time," but she stirs herself to get to the doors before the train stops. She likes Passy, such a peaceful civilised area after the bustling Latin Quarter, although she usually avoids the embassy district where there might be armed sentries in their lookout boxes. The new leaves are on the trees already with the blossom fading. They walk into the courtyard past the concierge, then up in the old wrought iron lift.

"You're very tired," Paula watches her drift across the room to her bed.

"Yes. It sometimes takes me this way," she folds on to it and closes her eyes.

She wakes to the smell of coffee. Paula has obviously decided it's time to move.

"Just what I need," Eleanor helps herself and stretches at the window. "What's the time?"

"Nearly eight. You slept for ages."

"Hungry?"

"Yes, I am rather."

"I need a shower. Then we're off." She stands under the water, soaking her head to wake herself up. Paula doesn't seem to have noticed anything, not even her need for a shower. She emerges with a large white towel around her head. Paula is standing at the window, gazing into the blue spring sky of the evening. She turns and grins at Eleanor. Enlightenment has dawned in her absence.

"I know what you were doing! I've just realised why you needed sluicing down. Post Marc, eh?"

"Indeed," Eleanor meets her friend's eyes with a laugh of delight. Perhaps it will be easy after all.

"Gosh I'm slow." Paula shakes her head while Eleanor towels her own roughly. "I've been in Rivertown too long."

"About time you left that all behind."

"Any good, is he?" Paula tries some new found sophistication.

"Not bad. You're right not to get too excited about Michel though."

"When they came up I thought they were both gay actually."

"You'll have to become more discriminating than that. The Parisian macho walk is not to be misinterpreted."

They laugh together and the years fall away once more. The room feels like their old flat in Auckland, discussing a student night out. Eleanor is as funny as ever, recalling and imitating voices from the past, making Paula laugh.

"Do you ever see any of those people now?"

"Not really. Names in the paper at times, or on books."

"We were part of quite a literary generation weren't we?"

"Pity it missed us."

"Not at all. There's still time."

"A whole summer in fact!"

"So what are you going to do with it? Write? Just relax?" Eleanor looks at Paula quizzically.

"Don't think I've got anything to say that hasn't been said already."

"Oh it's all been said, lots of times. But that's not the point."

"There aren't any original ways of saying it left either."

"It doesn't have to be profound or significant. Write poetry again. Do something self indulgent, that's why you're here."

"What about you?"

"I don't need to do anything. Just stopping work is self indulgent enough." Eleanor refills their coffee cups. Then she goes to the cabinet and finds the brandy bottle. "Time for an apéritif. In the coffee will do. One lump or two?"

Paula laughs and holds out her cup for a generous slosh of cognac. Eleanor takes a square lump of sugar from the bowl and holds a corner of it in her black coffee, watching the colour rapidly fill it before putting it in her mouth. Paula is fascinated, following suit. They sit and crunch sugar cubes of strong coffee and brandy, giggling competitively in the race to soak it up.

"Time we ate," Eleanor says at last, shifting the bowl further away. "What do you feel like?"

"Up to you. Are we meeting the others?"

"Not planning to. Served his purpose. On to something else," they laugh together again.

They talk long over a leisurely meal, staying in Passy.

"Haven't you ever indulged since you married?" Eleanor wants to push her small advantage.

"No. It hasn't really occurred to me."

"Until your raving Welshman?"

"No way was that possible. Not in Rivertown!"

"I thought that was just the right place, relieve the boredom."

"I couldn't." Eleanor realises that's the simple truth. Paula couldn't have.

"That's all worlds away now though. You don't even need to think about it."

"Don't think I'm ready for a casual hour in Paris though!"

"Come on! Not that casual. I've known him for years!" Eleanor defends herself, laughing. "Anyway, do you want to go on somewhere else tonight?"

"I don't mind. If you want to go off..."

"No. I don't. There's a place not far from here that has music. Not too strenuous with travelling tomorrow."

"I wouldn't mind a good sleep."

"Right. Just a drink or two, and there shouldn't be anyone I know."

There isn't. They sit over drinks in a darkened cellar, silent now with the music, enjoying just being together. They stroll back in the clear evening. The phone rings not long after, and Eleanor talks while Paula goes to bed. When she comes into the room Paula sits up.

"I don't mind if you..."

"Shut up silly Polly." She throws a pillow across the

93

room. "That's enough. He just wanted us to join them at some club and I said we were too tired. Pas de problème," and she gets quickly into bed, turning the light out.

It's already the second week in May as they drive down the Loire Valley. They stop as fancy takes them, enjoying the chateaux and the river. After three leisurely days they're on the south coast of Brittany, with its wooded river valleys, beaches and islands, old standing stones and characteristic architecture. There are ancient spires at the centre of each town or village, little wayside chapels or calvaries, distinctive stone or plastered houses with grey slate roofs. They fetch up in Quimper for two nights with more friends of Eleanor. Rémy and Anne-Marie both work in town, and live on the hill above where steep roads go down towards the river through winding streets, with the occasional modern apartment block. Their small garden is filled with lilac in bloom, the heavy scent of that and the wisteria on the fence filling their senses when they sit outside the stone pavillon, or semi detached house, in the evenings. From the guest room they look over the town, the river.

Eleanor takes herself off for several hours a day, leaving Paula to wander through the old cobbled pedestrian streets, the gallery and museum, the cathedral with the crooked nave and its king on horseback between the two unequal spires. Across one of the many bridges over the river, lined with trees and gardens, are cinema complexes where Paula finds two films, one in English with French subtitles to help her French.

"Don't get the wrong idea," Eleanor assures her on the second afternoon when they meet outside a café by the river for a glass of wine. "I'm not off doing it every five minutes, I'm actually sorting out some business here for a friend in London."

"Really," Paula raises her glass sceptically.

94

On a sunny day they finally drive back to the coast and into Concarneau around the corniche, with sails on a blue Atlantic and fishing boats finding the river entrance between the rocky bays and sandy beaches, the medieval 'ville close' with its stone ramparts hiding the street of tourist shops and crêperies.

Eleanor parks and takes her bag to check into a hotel, to Paula's amazement.

"I don't think the house will be ready. We'll go out in the morning and air it. It's been empty all winter and it'll probably be damp."

"Is it near the sea?"

"Near enough. A real New Zealander are you, not wanting to be too far from the sea?"

"Aren't you like that too?"

"Guess I am at base. Have to do without it quite a bit though."

"It'll be nice to go swimming."

"The Atlantic will still be a bit chilly. Later."

They sit outside the hotel's corner bar in the afternoon, looking across to the port, sipping muscadet.

"Feeling good Polly?"

"Oh yes. I'm loosening up already."

"Obviously. The echo of that harassed look you arrived with has finally disappeared."

"Harassed?"

"Yes, harassed. Haunted by the life you left behind."

"It's funny really. I'm not worrying about them at all."

"Nor should you. You can't do anything from here."

"Perhaps that's it. The greater the distance, the less I feel responsible."

"Must be strange, feeling accountable for other people."

"I can't imagine not being. Not really."

"Your lot are old enough to manage. Nobody really needs anybody else."

"You think so? I don't agree."

"Everyone thinks they can't get along without a mate of some sort, someone as a base security, to tie us down.

It's not true."

"But even you were thinking..."

"Oh I think from time to time. But I know I'm better off independent, with only myself to think about."

"What about that child you didn't have?"

"I'd never have coped with the responsibility. It wouldn't have been fair to a kid."

An old woman with a small dog and a large shopping basket takes the table next to them. As always, the chairs are facing out. The dog pulls on its lead to explore under their table, sniffing their shoes, before settling down under an empty chair. The woman chats with the young waiter as she orders a pastis, deploring the destruction of the old church that used to dominate the town's skyline. The new replacement is much smaller, its modern lines, supposed to represent a ship, do not have the presence of the old stone. Eleanor listens, nodding. She hates it too, wishing the original church could have been restored in spite of the expense. The woman includes her, they agree and commiserate while the waiter goes to fetch her drink.

Eleanor orders more wine when the waiter returns.

"Are you really planning to do nothing?" perhaps Paula's worried it might be boring.

"Maybe I'll paint."

"You paint?"

"Yes. Even took classes one summer when I had to stay in London."

"Any good?"

"Not bad. Got a bit of encouragement. Then I moved to Berlin and there wasn't any more time."

"Have you got your things?"

"Sketching stuff. Everything's available here though. Robert's a painter and photographer, the owner of the house."

"You can use his stuff?"

"He won't mind. He's on a magazine assignment in Africa, he mostly does photographic work."

"Maybe you can do enough for an exhibition at the

end of the summer."

"You must be joking."

"I dare you. I'll start writing again if you paint enough for an exhibition."

"For that I might."

"Here's to new careers for both of us!"

"Yec'hed Mad!"

"What's that?"

"Breton for 'cheers.'"

"You know some Breton?"

"Not much more than that. Don't ask me to spell it either!"

"When were you last here?"

"Last year. I stayed in the house we're going to." Not a shadow but a flash of light, a sudden illumination, passes over Eleanor's face. She sees Paula notice it and wipes it off.

"He's French?"

"Of course. Might turn up some time. Would you mind?"

"Why would I?"

"Oh you know, breaking into our peace," Eleanor turns to look at a boat coming in. She never was a blusher, but she can feel her cheeks warming a little under Paula's stare. "We must go shopping. Let's make a list," and she makes the rest of the afternoon practical.

Eleanor is proud the next morning when they drive several kilometres out into the country. She lines up the maximum effect to impress Paula. Robert's house is typically whitened stone with a steep grey slate roof, like the majority of houses they pass. It stands in a clump of trees, an old orchard. As with some of the others, the windows and doors are picked out with darker coloured bricks, but the shutters are all white. The jutting upper windows in the roof are open, and bedding billows on the sills. Eleanor smiles, pleased.

"Robert must have let Madame Guilvennec know we were coming.'

"How could she know the date when we didn't know

ourselves?" Paula looks at the fresh baguette on the table, the bowl of fruit, another of large brown eggs.

"I don't question second guessing. Perhaps it's been ready every day. On the other hand, I'm inclined to believe in sixth sense among the Celts, these Bretons."

"You?"

"Why not? Did you take me for a complete sceptic?"

"Suppose I did."

"I've always thought there was more to telepathy and transferring thought than we realised when we played at experimenting with it."

"Well yes. The mind is fascinating."

"Those eastern johnnys knew a lot more about it than the west I reckon."

"Confucius?"

"No no. He was too into the filial piety bit and all that duty stuff. Zen. Taoism. Indian mysticism. Much more interesting, and more in the mind."

"I don't know much about all that."

"Let me broaden your education then. You can read French. Robert has quite a good collection of books from when he was in the East."

"I can see there won't be much time for sight seeing."

"You're not a tourist Polly. Heaven forbid. We've done far too much of that already."

"It's been good though."

"You're here to soak up the real France now. You know all that tourist stuff."

"OK. Let the education begin."

"It's never stopped, idjit. Imbécile, as Robert would say."

"That doesn't sound kind."

"It's not. Apposite though. He's just."

"Just?"

"A good word. Not used enough."

"More learning."

They exchanges smiles of complicity. Eleanor feels good to have her old side kick back. It's going to be a stimulating summer.

Time passes easily at first. They spend leisurely mornings with coffee and croissants in the café of a tiny village within walking distance. If a late night makes them more hungry, they cook up their own substantial breakfasts with the big free range eggs of a vibrant gold Paula hasn't seen since her childhood days, and tasty freshly cured ham.

Madame Guilvennec, who lives at the closest farm, arrives several times a week with fresh eggs, ham, and fine looking greens from her garden. Sometimes she can be persuaded to sit and talk with them over a drink, telling the eager Paula local stories. She has to listen hard to understand Madame's local accent. She's quite a big woman, with working hands and a broad face lapsing into several chins, especially when she gives one of her full body laughs. Even when she is persuaded to sit for a while her hands stay busy, working at each other, or even at fine handwork she takes from the bottom of the large basket in which she brings the eggs or vegetables for them. Mostly she hurries back, or even sends a child over after school with the produce.

Between ten and eleven in the morning they both set to work. After the first two days a pattern develops. Eleanor finds an old easel which she puts up outside to paint the trees, the house, the glimpse of the sea by the Pointe de Trévignon. Paula sits at a rickety table in the shade and tries to write, but mostly she just reads and makes notes from books. Eleanor is quick and deft, as she is in most things. Her watercolours catch an unexpectedly live angle on what she sees.

"Can't catch people at all," she states to an admiring Paula. "But I'll have one shot at you. Take your book over to that wisteria."

The buzzing summer sounds increase. Already the rich wisteria flowers are fading from their vibrant purple blue. The summer begins with the heavy scents of lilac and mimosa echoing as the flowers fall. It's promising to be an aromatic sultry one, and they both feel sensuously alive in the heat of the still garden, with a pleasurably expectant feeling.

"Not missing your family now, are you."

"Goodness. I haven't even read that letter from Nora we picked up this morning." They started late after going in to the market, and Paula went to the Post Office to collect her mail and post some letters.

"What's she got to say?"

"I'll read it out.

> 'Dear Paula,
> How's it all going? Hope you're making the most of all the opportunities and thoroughly enjoying yourself. I think Miss Gray misses you a lot. Every time I go in she asks after you, even though she's shown me several cards from you and talked about the letter you wrote after visiting her friend. She has a teenager to help after school but she doesn't seem very pleased with her. She's always putting her right on what to do. She says today's students can't even add up two figures in decimal currency. I do so hope she's not right.
> The house in France sounds most pleasant. Gordon said you sounded very happy with it all when you rang. You must not buy things to send us though. I loved my scarf from Paris, it's beautiful and much admired, but you must get things for yourself, it's your holiday.
> Gordon took me to Simon's sports day. Simon was such a young gentleman when we took him out to dinner, hard to associate with the hot exhausted and triumphant sportsman we saw get second place running earlier on. He is still slight for his age but very speedy, and will no doubt do even better as he develops more. Such hefty boys some of them. His best friend came to dinner also, a farmer's son in the Manawatu. A new name to me, Malcolm, but perhaps you

know of him.

You'll be interested to know we won the petition. The supermarket is making its new car park in the swamp. We keep that charming little park.

Winter has settled in and I'm enjoying blazing fires with all that lovely wood Gordon cut for me, and all those good television programmes from the BBC that they so wisely save for winter evenings.

You will be well into summer now, after that beautiful spring you talked about. France sounds so lovely. Keep enjoying my dear, I think of you often.

with love,
Nora'"

"All good news then."

Eleanor has been concentrating on catching Paula's expression as she reads, adding a few more strokes.

"Yes. She certainly writes a more satisfying letter than the others."

"Well she's got time for the over view. Gordon's working and the kids are as self centred as most teens."

"Thought you didn't know much about kids."

"I notice. Even when I avoid them."

"Still haven't heard from Roz. I've written several times."

"Maybe she's not a letter writer. Some people just aren't."

"I thought she would have been."

"You just want news of that Welshman."

"Nonsense."

"Maybe she's performing with him and they're having an affair so she doesn't want to tell you."

"I don't really care what's going on there now."

"Good. Have a look at this."

"Wow. I'm not that sylph like and glamorous."

"Don't put yourself down." She's used delicate

101

pastels to give an ephemeral misty effect, and it's certainly flattering. It also helps conceal what she knows are big deficiencies in her figure drawing, but at least Paula seems pleased.

Eleanor has just about reached her threshold of capacity for daily painting. Something will have to happen soon or she'll start going potty. Their afternoon walks along the coast, the first swim, the local trips, are becoming tedious, while Paula still bubbles with excitement at everything they do, including her reading and the notes she makes. Now she's finally relaxed and let go all the work pressures, Eleanor feels expectant, ready for the next stage.

Chapter Twelve

Paula is loving every moment of their time. Just letting go of all the usual demands, turning off any sense of responsibility, has transported her into a new self awareness, a sense of pleasure at having nothing to think about except pleasing herself and Eleanor. She has never felt so hedonistic in her life. Even sitting in the garden each warm morning, watching Eleanor paint, seeing the bees and insects in the long grass, the trees, allowing herself to be frequently distracted from the books in front of her, is such an unforeseen indulgence. She's beginning to sense that Eleanor is getting restless. It worries her, she doesn't want anything to change. Her gaze fixes on the gnarled wood of an old apple tree which she can see Eleanor is trying to capture in paint, so that neither of them notices the diversion when it comes.

The large car pulls up silently, a voice calls to Eleanor in French. Car doors slam amid a hail of cheerful greetings. Paula looks startled, but Eleanor isn't surprised at all. She lazily puts down her brush and presents her face for the kisses, 'la bise', on each cheek.

As Paula slowly rises the voices, there are only three, switch quickly and easily to English.

"Don't worry. We're only passing. Robert said you might be here."

"You've seen him?"

"Laurent is just back from Africa, on his way to Spain. He saw him."

"What's Laurent doing in Spain?"

"Searching for some new artist."

"Here's a new artist for him," Catherine, the woman, has been having a closer look at Eleanor's work.

"Pas mal du tout," the second man, Jean-Pierre, comes over. "How long have you been painting?"

Eleanor dismisses it carelessly, but Claude picks it up to get better light on it.

"You've got something there. The way the figure's hair reflects the colour of the wisteria flowers falling, then you pick it up again with that glimpse of the sea."

"Yes. A good eye for colour."

"Keep going Eleanor. Could be a future in it," Claude puts it down again and puts his arm lightly around Eleanor's shoulders. Paula is impressed, noticing how he pronounces her name Eléanore caressingly, with a French accent. Claude is impressive. Quite tall and dark, with a casual air reflected in his black cotton pants, black t shirt, the easy confidence in all his movements. Jean-Pierre is heavier, his face echoes the Breton features, marked, with a strong profile, a heavy jaw, and receding hair.

By now Eleanor has got out some cooled muscadet and glasses and they sit around the outdoor table, one side in shade, the other in the sun, where the Parisians choose to lounge.

"Nothing quite like the warmth of a Breton summer."

"Shades of your childhood, Jean-Pierre?"

"Well it's always nice to come back."

"Can't throw off your roots for Paris?"

"It's not that. I couldn't live here now. Only visits."

The voices hum with the buzzing of insects, merging in the increasing heat to an agreeable blur, as Eleanor passes the second bottle around, adds some bowls of nibbles and leans back, closing her eyes. Paula looks from one to the other, remarking the easy conviviality. They talk of mutual friends, their decision to make a detour on their return from the south, having heard that Eleanor is back in France. Eleanor seems to be waking from a reverie, becoming more animated again, responding to her friends. Art and books are forgotten now.

Jean-Pierre looks at his watch. "It's lunch time. Well

past."

"We'll take you out. Come on." Claude stands, pulling Eleanor up from where she has sprawled on the grass beside him.

They all pile into Claude's car and drive off to a local restaurant. Claude parks in the main square of Concarneau and leads them to a restaurant at the side, looking out over the pleasure boats in the marina, by the river mouth. A table in the window is quickly prepared for five, the prix fixe menus surveyed and selected. Paula looks at the dark wood of the walls, the still life pictures, the heavy silver and fine linen. The tourists sit outside at the several more open restaurants along the square. Here the French dine in discreet comfort. She's in good company. She always is with Eleanor, whose taste for fine things she remembers even from their student days.

Jean-Pierre talks about his childhood on the coast not far from Robert's place, the fishing, the romances on the beach.

"That's not so different from my childhood in New Zealand," Paula exclaims with delight.

"We are the same everywhere," Jean-Pierre is both smug and magnanimous, turning his attention more on Paula as they make their comparisons. Paula opens up to this big teddy bear of a man, with his harsh voice belying his gentleness. Eleanor grins as she notices Catherine watching too, and they exchange looks of amusement. At some stage Paula will wonder which man has a connection with Catherine, and Eleanor is willing to lay the odds she won't get it right.

"So what are you writing?" Jean-Pierre is still quizzing Paula.

"I'm trying to write poetry, but I've only written a few scrappy pieces. I keep getting sidetracked with all the books here, making notes on totally irrelevant things."

"That's probably a good way to go about it. See where your inclinations lead."

"I'm enjoying it anyway. It's great having the

opportunity to do what I feel like doing."

"Away from your children. You must be very busy at home," the elegant Parisienne has been listening too. Paula admires the casual chic of her clothes, the gleaming black hair caught back behind her dainty ears with the chunky gold clusters. She could never look like that in a thousand years.

"You don't have children?"

"Yes. A son. He is with his father in Italy."

Eleanor rescues a gulping Paula. "Pierre is seventeen now. He helps his father making films in the holidays."

"He's making an Italian film?"

"Yes. They make many co-productions now. You may have seen a Philippe Noiret one."

"Wonderful. Did Stéphan work on that too?"

"No. They used an Italian camera man."

"What is Pierre doing?" Eleanor remembers the charming teenager from Paris.

"Bit of a gofer really, but he's learning the camera techniques. Stéphan didn't want him to follow the same path, but he's so determined, and very good already."

"He's going on studying then."

"Yes. It's nice when they grow up. I enjoy him so much more."

"I can't wait," Paula surprises herself with her response and Eleanor grins.

"You're doing the right thing anyway, sending them away to school. Speeds up the process. When do you go back to work?" Eleanor obviously doesn't want to talk of children. She switches them back to Paris.

"Next week. But then I'm off to a computer conference in Germany," Claude stretches back in the chair with his liqueur coffee.

"He's always on the road," Jean-Pierre taunts him. "No wonder he can't keep a woman."

"In the air actually," Claude is lofty. "And I'd rather they kept me."

"You should be so lucky!" Eleanor challenges him with her eyes.

"We'd make a good team, you and me. We could keep each other." Claude won't be squashed.

"Dream on. You won't find me waiting your frequent returns."

"You depart just as much yourself, you can't talk."

"Which is why I stay free too, stupid." Eleanor grins at him. It's obviously an old argument. Paula looks around the group again, thinking what a different world they all live in to hers. She finds it strange but stimulating that Eleanor is at home with so many disparate groups of people. Yet she can see how they all, from London through Paris to Brittany, more or less reflect her friend's tastes and attitudes. There's a sense of freedom about her life which is totally new to Paula.

"And you are trying your freedom this time?" Jean-Pierre brings the attention back to her.

"Not really. Just a holiday from my normal life."

"We all need that."

"She's so much more relaxed now. All that distance has a magical effect," Eleanor claims credit.

"A Breton summer is very relaxing. A release from family concerns," Jean-Pierre runs his fingers lightly down her bare arm and Paula shivers with self-conscious pleasure.

"It's not so bad as that," she murmurs. Eleanor at least doesn't believe her. She steers the conversation away from families again. Paula catches her eye, knowing what she's thinking, and grins. She does forget her family while she's here. She's been surprised at how easy it is.

Chapter Thirteen

Eleanor wakes in the morning feeling a little disgruntled and restless. Her friends moved on after lunch. They might call back later in the week after doing something else around Brest. She turned down an invitation to go with them. It felt like a good thing to do at the time. The morning after it feels like an unnecessary sacrifice. Perhaps the fine Breton misty rain that has set in has something to do with it. Then she chides herself for being uncharitable. She has a car, there's nothing to prevent her doing anything, Paula is very amenable. It must be PMT. She's getting older, it seems to creep up on her more violently these days. More indications of time's clock running out. She forces herself to get up, peeping in on a still sleeping Paula, before she puts the coffee on and has a shower

It's still raining and looks like continuing when she emerges. Visibility has receded. Paula stirs at the smell of coffee.

"Depressing when it gets like this." Eleanor pours two bowls and passes them to Paula who has heated the milk. They smother chunks of yesterday's baguette with huge spoonfuls of her favourite sinfully rich chocolate chestnut spread, to which Paula has taken with glee also, dunking them in the creamy coffee.

"Life's little luxuries," Paula refuses to look at the rain without sustenance. "Let's do something special today."

"Like what?" Eleanor's mouth is full with a second chunk of bread.

"We haven't been to the artist town to look for traces of Miss Gray yet."

"I suppose we could. I need some more paints,

Robert's blue is nearly all gone. I have to replace it at least."

"Must paint a lot of sea then."

"He does. That's his," Paula follows her eyes to the wall behind them and the turbulent blue oils. Most of the art work in the cottage is very good enlarged photographs, or classy reproductions, the small painting in the corner is easily overlooked.

"He's good. I mightn't have realised it was the sea if we weren't so close though."

"Pleb!" Eleanor laughs, finally loosening up to the gloomy morning. "Let's go then. Got any names to go on?"

"Just a gallery that Antonia thought should still be there."

The valleys are filled with mist as they drive the relatively short distance. Trees, or the typical grey steep roofs, jut at intervals.

"Taoist mist, in the valleys of enlightenment."

"You were going to tell me about that."

"Plenty of time. Here we are," Eleanor negotiates a narrow street of mostly galleries by a stream with stone houses and a water wheel, then she parks by the river with a stone footbridge and boats tethered on a risen tide. It's so picturesque, with a glimmer of sun beginning to part the mist, that Paula finds it unreal, like those preserved streets in English villages full of tourists.

"It's beautiful." The mist peels back up the slopes before them, revealing the timeworn stone on the other side of the narrowing river.

"Yes. It is rather. I need another coffee," Eleanor is more prosaic. She's seen it before. They walk back past the water wheel and over a stone bridge into the main square, where they sit outside and look at the map and pamphlets they pick up from the tourist office next door to the café. The rain has cleared, everything gleams and reflects in the new sunlight. The waiter puts extra tables and chairs outside the awning as more people arrive.

"It's always busy here. Look at that gallery owner over there, attracting the tourists."

They watch the activity for a while. A middle aged woman with long white hair sits at the table next to them, a large soft teddy bear peeping out of her small back pack which she places on the chair beside her.

"I'd like to be that eccentric," Paula whispers to Eleanor, delightedly watching the woman adjust the bear so he seems to be sitting at the table with her. Even the waiter makes a remark to it, which the woman misses.

"Only an American would be that mad, certainly not a local," Eleanor assesses the woman's clothes, not local either, the usual comfortable travelling loose pants and shirt.

"I'd like a teddy bear like that," Paula's thoughtful.

"I have several, but I don't travel with them."

"How did you get them?"

"The first one was given me by a rather lovely teddy bear of a man, when he had to go away. It seemed a good excuse to start a collection."

"I loved your one in London."

"You should have said. We could have brought him."

"I'm not serious."

"Why not? We should get you one if you have the urge."

"As a child substitute? Much less trouble."

"You're getting the idea. That's my family. Bears, all of them."

The woman notices their interest and smiles at them. She can't be English though, as she doesn't seem to understand their conversation. Or perhaps she chooses not to communicate with English speakers, Eleanor thinks, recognising something she does herself at times. She opens the map.

"What's the name of that gallery? Let's see if it's here."

"Galerie Suzanne."

"A woman?"

"Is that so rare?"

"Yes, actually."

It's on the list, and they set off up the road past the major town art gallery.

"We'll go in there on the way back."

"There's the sign," Paula looks up the hill as they turn a corner.

It's only small. They push open the door into a crowded room with all the walls full of pictures, and more framed work stacked against them. There's nobody there. They look around for a while, with still no sign of the owner. They try knocking on the counter, almost hidden beneath piles of prints and papers. They cough, talk loudly, still nothing. The door to the back of the shop stays firmly closed.

"Maybe we should come back later," Eleanor's ready to give up.

Then the street door bursts open and a woman comes in. She greets them warmly, and it's a moment before they realise she's not just another customer. She apologises for not being there, she had to run down to another gallery to deliver a painting. Eleanor notices the framing samples on the wall behind the counter, realising the business is perhaps more framing than selling art. In that case it doesn't matter being a little out of the way from the other tourist galleries.

Paula starts explaining her mission. Eleanor helps a little with her French, while the woman patiently listens.

"No, I would not have been here," she tells them. "It is too long ago. You need Madame Suzanne. She is retired now. I took over from her." She gives them an address, then telephones and arranges for them to visit.

"You are lucky. She is at home. So often she is not. Such a busy retirement!" She shakes her head and smiles. She is obviously busy herself. They walk back with the address, looking on the map to find it's just the other side of the main street, above the river.

As they stroll up the narrow road they turn and

savour the view, across the river to the wooded hills, high enough to not even see most of the tourist street.

Madame Suzanne Perec has been weeding her flourishing garden, she's just picking up her fork and gloves when they arrive. She's small and neat, with intelligent black eyes and her grey hair cut short and unwaved, unlike many French women of her age. Eleanor decides she was once a beauty, perhaps even much painted. Her conjecture is confirmed when they're led inside. There's a large portrait in the hallway of the stone cottage that is unmistakably those eyes, shining with fresh youth, smooth white shoulders above the ball gown. Madame notices her studying it in the brief pause while she puts down her gardening things and opens another door.

"A salutary reminder of how long ago it all was," she smiles at them, mirroring the half smile in the painting. Eleanor wonders if she knows, or if she only sees her wrinkles and age marks. Perhaps she knows, that beauty shadowed. She makes no concessions to trying to retain it though, however self aware she might be.

They sit down in a lovely room crowded with a life time's memorabilia, good art works on the walls and tables, photos on the narrow mantel, fresh flowers everywhere. Madame clears papers off several chairs, the curve of wood and shades of tapestry from another century revealed. Paula is almost too nervous to sit on it.

They explain again.

"Oh yes. I remember la Néo-Zélandaise. But she only came here one season."

"I thought she made regular visits, for several years. Every summer."

"Yes. But she only spent one trip here. After that she preferred the coast."

"Do you know where she went?" It is Eleanor who asks.

"To Bénodet. You know it?"

"It's at the river mouth down from Quimper, isn't it?'

"That's right. A little resort town. She brought me some paintings from there."

"You sold her work?"

"Oh yes. It was quite competent."

"Would you have any?"

"Not now. Let me get you a drink while I think who might have bought one."

Paula eagerly follows the conversation, looking at Eleanor, pleased and excited.

"They did not come to Pont Aven so often once they went to Bénodet. They had no car."

"They?" Paula pounces on the French plurals.

"Yes. You did not know?"

"No."

"Perhaps he did not go to New Zealand."

"Who was he?"

"An artist also I think. No, perhaps not. I have forgotten the name. It will come to me."

"They were married?"

"I did not ask," there is a slight reproof in the words, and Eleanor approves. Not a good question. Paula is too eager. She puts a restraining hand on her arm and takes over again.

"Our friend was always shy about her painting. She wouldn't talk about it," she claims Miss Gray as hers too for the moment.

"She had no need to be. Not brilliant, but good enough. She could have kept going, learned more. She had a good eye."

"Do you know why she stopped?"

"The last season. I think she came alone. Yes. Guillaume." She says the name thoughtfully, the English William sounding so much more romantic in French. "That was the name. She said Guillaume had to go early, return to Ireland. She was going there too, I think."

"Do you know where she stayed in Bénodet?"

"I had the address. She asked me to send painting things at times." She goes to the desk in the corner and

113

pulls out several notebooks, turning pages.

"Here it is," she writes it down for them. Then she takes their phone number in case she remembers who might have a painting of Miss Gray's. She will look in the books at the shop, but she suspects the new manager may have got rid of some of the old invoices, they take up so much space.

Paula obviously can't believe her luck. She quivers with questions. Eleanor can see it's time to stop. She talks of other things, discussing local art, the changes in the village which Madame deplores, although she's realistic about the need for tourists. A good business woman, Eleanor thinks, feeling she would like to know this forthright woman better.

"You have time to walk in the Bois d'Amour?" she asks them. "Now the day is so nice it will be lovely. Gauguin painted there," she tells Paula. "You could find the chapel with his Yellow Christ too. It's still there."

They thank her warmly. It's time to leave. Eleanor gives a last regretful look around the comfortable room, holding Madame's hand warmly as they say goodbye. Paula bubbles with excitement and can't wait to talk about it.

"Let's go up to the Chapel. We're nearly there, and we can walk back along the river through the trees and stones where he painted," Eleanor firmly leads her off. She insists they not go straight to Bénodet as Paula would like. It would be a waste of a trip where they are, with a good restaurant for lunch, a chance to look at the town gallery, then the new Gauguin gallery by the river. None of his work in it, although the main gallery has a room of painters from the Gauguin school.

In the afternoon the sky clouds over again, and mist snakes back up the valleys as they drive home.

"That was worth while then," Eleanor feels refreshed by a day away.

"She can't have been married. She would have stayed Mrs," Paula has no room for any other thoughts.

"Scandalous, huh! You think she ran away from a

shady past?"

"I wonder why she hid it all, the writing, the painting."

"Must have felt pretty bored in your town after all this," Eleanor feels increasing sympathy for Miss Gray. She must be some kind of victim of circumstance. The mystery has caught her imagination now too, especially after reading the travel book. She would like to see a painting, perhaps even a painting of her. Artists so often used each other as models.

Naturally Paula wants to go straight to Bénodet in the morning. Eleanor doesn't mind. She has plans of her own that will fit in. She does insist they work in the morning first. She's afraid Paula will be so over excited she'll blow the interview, as she nearly did with Madame Suzanne.

"Write about it. Get everything you know down on paper, then you'll have a better idea of the gaps," she assures Paula, after her protests that she can't possibly sit down and write in the morning. It's only when she gets out the painting things that Eleanor realises she completely forgot to get any more of that particular blue she wanted. Never mind. If the day goes as she hopes she'll be able to at some stage.

They pack up early, in time to drive off and reach the seaside resort for lunch.

"We can't possibly call on anyone till mid afternoon." Once again they sit with maps and pamphlets spread in front of them.

"I haven't even seen the sea yet," Paula protests at the choice of restaurant in the town centre.

"But this is good, isn't it. And we can leave the car here and walk right around the point. You'll like it. The street goes off the waterfront anyway."

"Can't we go now?"

"Give them a chance to finish eating. Lunch is the most important meal of the day, especially since they'll be retired."

"That's if they're both still there."

"Yes. Madame Suzanne didn't seem to know them, and it's such a long time."

"I'm glad I did do that writing. I feel much clearer now."

"You needed to come down out of the trees and touch ground again," Eleanor grins at her affectionately.

They walk down to the river, with its landing place for the cruise down from Quimper past the old chateaux and manor houses. A huge modern road bridge spans the water in a deceptively fragile looking arch, carrying the road further west. Many yachts and boats are moored along both banks. The walking path curves around past houses and little bays, with two prominent light houses on the points. Eleanor loves their phallic jutting, but she refrains from pointing it out to Paula. One is even called Le Coq. Then they reach the main promenade, facing out to the Atlantic. Paula exclaims at the sweeping expanse of white sand below the sea wall, and the row of wooden bathing huts that she still finds so incongruous right on the beach. Eleanor is satisfied with her reaction. Paula is looking at the street signs past all the hotels and cafés.

"Here it is."

"Why don't I leave you to it this time?"

"Oh no. I need your help."

"No you don't. You've put all the questions before."

"But what will you do?"

"I'd like to pop up to Quimper and get that paint I forgot, and a couple of other things."

"You're deserting me?"

"I'll come to the door if you like, then I'll be off. Let's meet at that café on the corner there, about six o'clock. There's plenty to look at here."

"If you must. Wish you'd come though," Paula is reluctant, but she's not going to relinquish her quest, with or without Eleanor.

A middle aged woman answers the door, looking at the paper Paula holds out with the names and address on it.

"C'est ma mère," she says, taking it and staring at the words as if they might reveal something extra to her. "Mon père est disparu il y a quelques ans. Attendez un moment. Elle est très fragile," and she goes inside, leaving them on the doorstep.

"I'll go now," but Paula clutches her arm until the woman returns.

"Yes. She would like to see you. She remembers Virginie very well," she gives the name the French pronunciation. Eleanor talks to her in fluent French for a few moments, explaining. Then she reminds Paula not to tire the old lady by staying too long, in English the woman does not follow, and leaves.

She takes the quick route through the central streets back to the car as Paula disappears into the house. As she drives off she smiles to herself. She doesn't hold out any great hope that Paula will find a dramatic solution to her mystery. She suspects that fragile elderly ladies have smudged recollections of twenty-five years previous.

It feels good to be on her own for a while. She parks near the centre of Quimper and walks through to a gallery to get her paints before she forgets again. Then she goes up the stairs beside one of the central tourist shops, on past the first floor crêperie and up to knock on a door with a discreet plate for a notary's services. It's her turn to vanish into a set of rooms.

When she emerges over an hour later she's accompanied by Rémy. They go into the nearest café and sit talking over an apéritif. It's some time before Eleanor glances at her watch and remembers Paula. It's already after six.

"I'll have to go," his hand holds hers across the table.

"Not yet. We could dine," he protests. "I often work late." She's sure he does.

"I can't leave her stranded in Bénodet."

"You're a mother then?"

"Not me. Never that, as you know."

"Your past will catch up with you."

"It already has. Many times."

"And you cope magnificently."

"Cope?"

"Prosaic I know. You soar above. Sublimely."

"Not so sublime. Soaring sounds a bit breathless for me."

"Remember Chamonix?"

"You taught me to ski."

"There you soared. You became so good so quickly."

"Like flying. It's been several years now."

"Next winter. We must rendezvous, you and me."

"It won't be the same."

"It will be better. I promise you."

"And Anne-Marie?"

"She has not told you. She is pregnant at last. The test was just this week. I think she will not be skiing next winter, but she will not prevent me from going."

"You a father. Hard to imagine."

The sleek Frenchman preens himself, letting go her hand to smooth back the immaculate dark hair, the first distinguished touches of white at the temples. "I will be a good father." He is very sure of himself.

Eleanor thinks of the days at the ski fields before his marriage, the third or fourth rendezvous when the group included Anne-Marie. A late marriage, a late father, full of the pride of his achievements. She has no regrets for the time she turned him down, watching him switch his attentions to the newcomer. She would not have fitted into his life plan, into Quimper as his wife. She still enjoys visiting them both, snatching the odd little moment with him, but that's all.

She strikes a lot of traffic on the route to the coast, so it's nearly seven when she finally reaches the café. Paula's looking a little despondent. Her face lights up as Eleanor walks in. It's still sunny, and will be light until after ten. Paula is impressed with the long summer evenings in Europe. They usually eat outside.

"I need a coffee first," she stems the torrent of words

118

Paula is all geared up to release.

"I couldn't have another coffee, I've had four," a slight reproach at her lateness.

"So much traffic," sufficient apology without expanding. "Why don't you have an apéritif?"

"I haven't tried pastis yet, and they all seem to drink it."

"You be careful. It's lethal. Put loads of water in it."

"I notice they bring bottles of water with it."

"Carafes, pleb."

"I want to taste the aniseed."

"It'll take more than water to drown the taste. It's really strong."

The waiter leaves their drinks. Eleanor agrees to his suggestion of a brandy on the side, tipping most of it into her coffee.

"I think we should eat here before driving back. I need a feed."

"Here?"

"No, silly. That restaurant we passed near the corniche. In the hotel."

"Great. I could see the dining room right over the beach."

"Yes, it's all open to the sea."

"You look satiated. Have you been off doing it again?"

"Perceptive Polly."

"I don't think I could cope with all those different bodies. Do you all the time?"

"I couldn't cope with the same body all the time. Don't you get bored?"

"How long have you lived like that?" Paula is not admitting to boredom yet, although the recognition of it lodges in her mind.

"Just about all my life."

"You mean when we were students?"

"You didn't know? Don't look so shocked."

"I didn't. Really."

"Small town innocent. You were the rare bird in those days."

119

"So what do you do now it's not safe to just take the pill? Do you look after yourself?" Paula worries and Eleanor grins.

"You forget the French practically invented the condom, the French letter."

"Is it really safe? Against Aids?"

"Of course. Anyway, I do choose my men more carefully than you seem to imply."

"Choices."

"Yes Polly. We all choose, and live with the results of the choices we make." Eleanor sucks on a coffee soaked sugar cube reflectively. She wonders if Paula is ready to make a deliberate choice, if the unease she has confessed with her situation will come to a head this summer now the world is opening up to her. It's time Paula stopped drifting through life letting her choices be made for her, by her family, by Gordon. If all she achieves this summer is to make her friend think for herself it will be something, she doubts if Paula will do anything radical. Then she thinks of the choices she has made herself, wondering if they really were carefully considered, or if they were random decisions dictated by events at the time.

Paula is looking pensive too.

"I've been thinking a lot about choices lately."

"It's probably time you did."

"I feel as if I've just drifted along most of my life, let things happen to me."

"Oh you chose. You chose the security of Gordon, the escape to domesticity in a small town."

"Did I?"

"Yes. You chose not to go solo out into the world and seek a career, like me."

"I always admired your strength, your independence. I never had the confidence."

"There you go again. Dropping out. It's rubbish. You were bright enough to do anything you wanted to."

"I suppose it's too late now."

"Not for you it's not. You could do anything."

"A lot of people are going back to studying now. They do extra mural courses from Massey University in Palmerston North."

"There you are then. Do another degree, do a masters, do something, Polly."

"I think I will. I hadn't considered it before."

Eleanor sees a new determination in Paula's face and she's pleased, delighted to join with her in speculation on what she might do next.

"With the kids away you don't need to do it extra murally. Why don't you spend a year or so in Auckland and get that masters you didn't do when you got engaged to Gordon?"

"That sounds a bit radical."

"Be radical. It's high time."

"I suppose the holidays would fit in with the children."

"You've grown out of small town life and drama clubs. Move on Polly."

"Not sure I want to be that revolutionary."

"Have some more pastis. You might."

"It's nice. I always like aniseed."

"Well don't go getting addicted. Come on. You can tell me about your visit over dinner."

"I'd almost forgotten."

"You were bursting with it when I came in."

They stroll along the waterfront. There are many promenaders in the balmy evening, full café terraces, late swimmers breaking the smooth surface of the unusually calm sea, families spreading picnics on the beach, still sunny. Other worlds seem far away, especially the antipodean islands to which Eleanor knows she will never return. She almost envies Polly again, her secure life back there, that will continue whether or not she leaves it to do a degree, whether or not she stays with Gordon. Polly will always be secure, one way or another. Eleanor thinks of the fleeting moments in her own life when that seemed possible, knowing that now it is irrevocably impossible. She shakes the thoughts out of her brain. It's Polly's day. She must respond to her excitement, get caught up in the quest of someone else's past again. A good way to go. They enter the restaurant, and are seated at a table looking out to sea. They both gaze at the distant horizon frequently during the meal, the paté and the coq au vin, the very good cheese board and the tarte au citron. They're full of their own thoughts for a while. Half way through the meal Eleanor finally steers the conversation away from the delicious food and wine, and their brief amusing discussion about the provenance of some of the guests at other tables.

"You've contained yourself well. Now tell me about the visit."

"Madame Guéguin wants me to go back some time. She's going to look for some photos she couldn't find today."

"That daughter looked pretty efficient."

"They have a lot of things stored in the attic apparently. And Madame Hugo was making tea."

"Relation of the poet?"

"I don't think so."

"Not a very poetic looking person."

"Her mother was. Frail and tiny, but as alert and with it as Madame Perec. Pity they didn't know each other. They would have got on well."

"Go on. Who was he?"

"He was Irish. They came back for four summers, two to three months each time. They didn't actually stay with Madame Guéguin. She owns the house next door, which is divided into self contained rooms. They rented one, the upstairs front, with a glimpse of the sea."

"So tell me about him."

"I'm beginning to feel a bit guilty. Bit as if I'm prying into something I shouldn't know."

"Well you are, if Miss Gray never said anything. But you don't need to tell her."

"He was a musician. Madame Guéguin said it was absolutely magic when he played the pipes, the flute.

122

She always wanted to dance, and Miss Gray would dance a little with him while he played."

"Sounds wonderful. What was his name?"

"She couldn't remember it. O'Flute or something like that, but she said herself she may just be confused with the English for his instrument."

"Fancy your Miss Gray. A wild Irishman."

"He was huge, apparently. With a beard."

"And no doubt all the Irish charm and bewitching ways," Eleanor is pensive, remembering an Irishman she knew for a while. Poor Miss Gray. She identifies with her, sympathising. How could she have ended what was obviously such a magical time in her life? There must be some tragedy, the man must be dead, surely.

"They would go back to the south of Ireland, on Bantry Bay she said. Miss Gray showed her paintings she did of it. Stones on a mountain side, she remembered, and a lake at an incredible altitude, just above the bay."

"Sounds magic. Ireland is, you know."

"You've spent time there?"

"Yes, in Cork, but travelling round a bit too. I know your bay. It has quite a French connection. A French oil tanker or rig or something exploded there once, big loss of life. It's a huge deep water cove."

"They didn't spend all the time there though. He had a cottage somewhere, then they, or Miss Gray at least, would go back to England. She thought they sometimes met in the south of France too, from what they said, and Miss Gray's paintings."

"What a super life. How could she leave it to go back to New Zealand?"

"That's what I'm wondering. Must have been something dramatic, tragic."

"Guess you'll never know unless you dare to ask her."

They both look out to sea again, thinking of Miss Gray, of the past. Eleanor is nostalgic. There are magical times in her own past, gone beyond recall. No doubt

Miss Gray is wise not to have returned, to have escaped to her sheltered book shop in a small town with her private memories she does not share. Sensible woman. Is it because Paula does not have such a magical past that she is so fascinated by this story? She smiles to herself, wondering how open Paula would be to such an escape from her life. She wouldn't dare try to arrange it, but she can't help thinking it's just what Paula needs.

Paula hasn't noticed her smile, her speculation. She's returning to her account of the afternoon.

"Madame called her Virginie all the time. It sounded like an entirely different person."

"It probably was. Must have changed altogether to make that switch back."

"Wish I knew what happened."

"Your Madame Guéguin has no idea?"

"No. One summer they came, said they'd be back the next, and all she got was a little note from Miss Gray to say that she was unable to return, she was going back to New Zealand."

"She never wrote again?"

"Christmas cards for a few years, but never with any news other than to say she had a bookshop. They knew that."

"No word of her Irishman?"

"No. He never wrote."

"Well, that seems about the limit of your detection. Mystery solved?"

"I suppose it is. Nice to know she had a few memorable summers."

"Can you say something to her when you get back?"

"I thought about that while I was waiting for you. Maybe I could say I met Madame Perec through you, talk about her painting, see if she'll say anything."

"She might be more likely to if you said you'd met Madame Guéguin. Then she'd know you'd heard about the Irishman."

"Oh dear. It does seem a bit mean, poking in her past behind her back."

Eleanor wonders if Paula's curiosity is finally sated, or if she will want to know even more. There is a pause while their plates are changed. They watch a yacht sailing across the bay towards the river mouth, leaning into the wind. People are packing up now, leaving the beach as the light fades. A lone child is being called from a last paddle as the tide recedes.

"I can't go any further without his name anyway." Paula stirs her coffee. "Madame Guéguin said it could be on one of the photos, so I might learn more."

"That'll be fun, finding out what he looked like." Eleanor is intrigued by this Irishman. A William sounds prosaic, but he can't have been, not a flute player who gave Miss Gray her amazing summers so long ago. But Paula is not thinking of him.

"I'm more interested in what she looked like then. I can't imagine the Miss Gray I know doing any of these things."

"What, painting or wild Irish affairs?"

"Either really. Just living in all these exotic places."

"You're sure it's the same person?"

"Oh yes. Madame Guéguin had a copy of Miss Gray's travel book on the shelf. It was inscribed to her, she showed me. In French too. I didn't know she spoke French."

"Another secret. Quite a lady, your Miss Gray."

"Madame wasn't sure if it was him on the trip though."

"So how did you explain your questions?"

"I said I worked for Miss Gray and was following her connections through Europe. It's true, it all followed on from Antonia in London."

"Always best to stick to the truth, or suitable portions of it." Eleanor is amused at Paula's still doubtful expression. The waiter hovers, they've already had two coffees, and she's ready to drive home at last.

"No more," she tells him, turning down a liqueur yet again. "The bill, please."

They're both thoughtful and silent driving back to the

house. It's late and the roads are not busy. The night is clear with no sign of the earlier mists. They pass small villages with just a few lights, curves of the road with glimpses of water inlets and looming moored boats, wooded valleys with an occasional lit farmhouse. Then through Concarneau, over the bridge past the old chateau up the valley and they're nearly home.

The house is dark and still when Eleanor turns off the car lights. She fumbles with the key and sees a note pushed into the crack of the door. They go in and she looks at it under the hall light, then grabs Paula's arm to stop her going in to turn on more lights.

"Hush. He's here," she's beaming with pleasure, tiredness vanquished, her eyes luminous.

"Who?" Paula is puzzled.

"Robert," Eleanor breathes the word like a mantra, rolling the French pronunciation, her r's like a caress.

"Where?" Paula looks around blankly in the half light from the hall shining into the living room.

"He says he's going to sleep in the attic, so as not to disturb us. He's just flown in and he's exhausted, so he got a car from Lorient. He'll be long asleep. We'll see him in the morning."

They go up silently to their rooms on the first floor, more than ready for bed. Eleanor has a shower, then lies awake, waiting for Paula to fall asleep. A little while later she creeps up the second flight of stairs, grateful for the sound deadening carpet, not so common on attic stairs. The door is ajar, a small night light burns by the old iron frame bed where the occupant turns, opens his eyes and holds out his arms to her. She crawls in beside him and snuggles up sleepily, safe, secure, the nearest to home she can get.

Chapter Fourteen

Roz feels guilty. It's her own fault. She looks at the letters and cards from Paula, remembering the times she's tried to write, the words that wouldn't come.

How could she?

How could she have?

It's no use having regrets now. It's too late. It was too easy. It's only now that the complications hit her. She hadn't given any thought to the way she would act afterwards, the way she would feel.

What will she say to Paula?

She went to Australia with Bill and the boys, then when they went on the outback trip Nora put Emma on the plane to meet her in Sydney. The two of them spent several days doing the sights and the shops. It was fun. Emma made no demands, being an agreeable and amenable companion. They flew back together while Bill and the boys were still away, and it was natural for her to join for meals with both Nora and Gordon while Emma was there. It was a treat to have a daughter for a while. It made the all male household feel a bit like an imposition. Emma made her miss Paula all the more.

Then term began. The next play started rehearsals and she agreed to take the lead role, opposite Gareth. Ian, another teacher, was producing it, and they rehearsed at his place. His wife Margaret had a cameo part too. It was strange acting without Paula. They still stopped on for coffee to talk after rehearsing. They all remarked on the gap Paula left and kept asking for news of her. Roz wished she had written earlier, instead of leaving Emma to pass on all the news about the trip. It would have been easy then. Why did she put it off?

Gareth was as attentive and friendly as ever, flirting beyond the stage, hamming up the romantic aspects of the play on it. It was pleasant, Roz bloomed in the attention. She started joining all the teachers for Friday night drinks in the bar, relaxed and convivial. So often Bill seemed to be working late, though he would join her later, then take fish and chips home or have a bar meal. Gordon started coming in too, joining them to be teased about his freedom.

Then Bill went away to a conference. She decided not to go with him, it would have been too difficult to get time away from teaching. She knew how hard it was to get relievers in the winter term. Besides, she had play rehearsals, and since the conference was in Christchurch Bill planned to take a few extra days to go skiing with some friends from there. She had lost her confidence skiing after breaking a leg badly when the boys were small. It was easier not to take it up again. Safer for her leg too, apparently, though it didn't stop her from doing anything else.

Bill left on a Tuesday night. She drove him to the nearest airport town, getting back in time for rehearsal. Gareth immediately started teasing her about being on her own for a week, no husband, a chance to play up. She fended him off calmly, amusing the others. She heard that Ben had been away in the holidays and met up with Barbara, who was now having an extended visit with relations in Australia. It was rumoured Ben might join her there some time, but no-one was saying anything.

"All these men for you to choose from." Gareth made play of her opportunities. "A whole week with Bill away."

"It doesn't seem to occur to any of you men that I might actually enjoy a few days on my own, without a man around to make demands on me."

"Hear hear!" Margaret applauded her. "Why don't you go away Ian?"

"I haven't had a home cooked meal in ages," Gareth

was still laying it on.

"I'm having a holiday from cooking. Luxury to only have myself to think about." Roz felt no urge at all to cook for him.

"Serve you right. You can cook for yourself," Margaret was tactfully not pointing out the times Gareth had eaten at their place.

"Nobody to light the fire for me when I come home." He was standing close to the big old fireplace with logs blazing, resting his coffee mug on the mantel.

"You should be the one who lights the fires. Ian does."

"But I've no-one to light them for."

"I'm off. See you Thursday," Roz ignored his plaintive pleas and hugged Margaret. Naturally he followed her out to the car, but she strapped herself in and would have driven off with the door open if he hadn't finally closed it, his lilting persuasions silenced in the cold night. She chuckled as she drove, thinking of the time she had driven off with Paula, leaving Gareth, or Ben, whoever it was, standing. However tempted she might be she would have more sense than to indicate any interest in front of the whole group. Surely Gareth must know that. He was far too up front in his pursuits. It ruled him out really, she couldn't be sure of his discretion without better indications than that.

The next rehearsal was similar. As usual she got away without Gareth after the practice, but when she was home in the empty house it suddenly seemed very empty indeed. Why on earth was she being so good? It was a bit pointless really. Goodness knew what Bill got up to on skiing trips with his old friends. He'd been going off without her for years now. She'd always been so good and boring, while he went away and had fun. Short trips with Paula and the children were not much compensation. If he took the boys skiing he always sent them back early so he could go on the main runs himself.

She was feeling deprived. Deprived of Paula. Deprived of fun. Staying home by herself and being dreary.

Friday night at the pub she drank a little more than usual to console herself. Gareth hung around her, Ben and Ian came to the table, other teachers. She flirted a bit more outrageously than usual, enjoying the reactions. Gordon came in, quite late, and that made her self conscious again. She quietened down as he came over and joined them.

"Any news of Bill?"

"One phone call. It's tonight he's off to the ski-field so I don't expect to hear again."

"He'll probably break a leg," Gareth hadn't stopped provoking.

"Not Bill. He's far too good," Gordon was dismissive of the idea.

"No. Only I do that," Roz sounded bitter and Gordon was immediately apologetic, buying her another drink.

"Think I need food more than that," she said as it came.

"Let's take it through and eat," Gordon offered.

Gareth started up at that, but Ian caught his arm.

"Remember you're coming home to tea with me," he reminded him. "Margaret took pity on you after your complaints the other night," he winked at Roz and took Gareth off. She went through with Gordon. They sat talking late over the meal.

It was the first time she'd ever really had Gordon to herself. She found it stimulating. He ordered a good bottle of wine with the meal, and on top of what she'd already had, she knew it was making her talk too much. Gordon just smiled and made gentle responses as she raved on. He carefully did not react to any complaints about being on her own while Bill went skiing, just took her hand in his big warm one and stroked her fingers, while he added brandy to her coffee and called for the bill.

She knew it would not be wise to drive, letting

Gordon put her in his car while he checked that hers was all right. She stumbled when she got out, so he took her arm up the path, unlocking the door when she fumbled with the keys. He came in and they stood in the dimly lit hall, looking at each other, his arm still holding her. She never knew whether it was the wine, the loneliness, or just that warm huggable man standing there in all his sympathetic niceness, but the tears started rolling down her cheeks. He took her in his arms to wipe them away, and she stayed there in the comfort of his bulky jersey and hard shoulder, snuggling into the warm skin of his neck until he pulled her head back and began kissing her properly.

The guest room was downstairs, just through the door, and they fell on to the bed together. Before she lost herself in the pleasure of the moment, her last fleeting thought was that they had both been deserted, so it was only justice that they comfort each other.

In the cold light of the next morning she woke to the empty bed and the realisation of what she had done. She had been sleepily aware when Gordon slipped away after seeing her to sleep. How would he be feeling?

She refused to even think about it. She was not prepared to change a thing. Why should she have regrets? She'd never even thought about Gordon in that way, he'd just been Paula's husband, Bill's friend, a good sort, her friend too, naturally. It was his initiative, but she'd enjoyed it so much she'd chosen not to stop. So who was responsible, and did it matter? She turned over and went back to sleep.

The telephone woke her late in the morning, and as she reached for it she hesitated, thinking it would be Bill. Then she reminded herself he would have been on the ski field long before, and picked it up.

"How are you feeling this morning?" Gordon's voice broke into her thoughts unexpectedly, with a new resonance and significance. She heard his breath in the pause while she collected herself.

"Only I wondered," he was giving her more time, she realised, "whether you felt like a drive today?"

"Fine. I'm not doing anything. Should we?"

"Why not?" Gordon was calm, natural, reassuring. "If you like, I thought we could go away for the weekend."

"Go away together?" She was stunned, looking down at her night dress, remembering Gordon putting it on her the night before. He was so kind, so gentle. She felt so good, better than she had in ages.

"I thought we'd go to this lodge I know. They have hot springs, great in the cold weather."

"Sounds wonderful."

"It is. Just what you need to relax. I'll pick you up around twelve."

She looked automatically at the bedside clock radio as he hung up, not giving her a chance to protest any more. Perhaps he knew she wasn't going to. It was far too tempting. She felt like being looked after, carried off. Her body still felt pampered, loved, awakened, at the thought of him. She had an hour and a half. She leapt up with renewed energy, showered and shampooed at leisure, paid attention to all the details of makeup and manicure she'd been neglecting with Bill away, chose her nicest clothes and night wear to put in a small bag. She was ready and waiting when Gordon drove up right on time.

She was suddenly self conscious about carrying her bag out to the car, but Gordon just took it.

"We're old friends, the neighbours see us coming and going all the time. I could be just taking you to the bus or anything."

He was right of course. There was no reason why they shouldn't be seen together. Then she remembered.

"My car!" They looked at each other and laughed.

"Just as well you remembered. That would have set the talk going!" as they drove down to pick it up.

She put the car in its garage while he followed her back up. Then they were off. Bother the neighbours! She would much rather it hadn't been Gareth crossing the road as they drove past the corner store though. His hand raised in greeting paused for a moment before continuing, as he saw who was in Bill's car. She pushed him right out of her mind. She could handle Gareth, no trouble.

"Don't be nervous," Gordon reached across and took her hand. "Nothing to worry about. This place is very discreet, I rang them. No-one we know booked in at all."

"You've been there before?"

"Oh yes."

"Paula's never mentioned..." the words died on her lips as he gave her hand a squeeze and turned with a grin. Obviously Paula had never been there. There was more to Gordon than she had ever thought. Her sudden question to herself as to what she was doing there, in the car with her best friend's husband, stayed inarticulate in her mind. She knew exactly what she was doing there. In fact she wanted to be there, she wanted to find out more about this suddenly exciting man she had known for so many years and never really noticed at all.

She did not ask any questions. Gordon made no explanations. The hot pools washed away all her doubts, Gordon swept away all the tension and loneliness she'd been feeling. It seemed so long since she had been the real centre of anyone's attention and she basked in it. Now she understood what sudden passion meant. From the hot pools to their king size bed she couldn't keep her hands off Gordon, and his hands were all over her, bringing her alive in a way she had forgotten was possible. Her every nerve ending tingled and cried out for more, as if sensually starved. They hardly stopped to eat. On the brief occasions that her mind actually left the thrill of the present moment, she allowed her suspicions of what Bill did on skiing trips to become a justifying certainty, telling herself that the freedom Paula was enjoying away from home, would have equally loosened her to temptation.

They drove back, surfeited, late on the Sunday night.

"You enjoyed yourself then?" He put her bag down in the hallway while she poured him a last drink.

"Great," she gave him a hug, then he pulled away and took the drink she was nearly spilling.

"Guess that's it. Bill back in a couple of days."

She looked at him in shock. She had not expected the end to come so soon, so finally, although she knew it had to come. She stayed silent.

"You're not going to tell him!" now it was Gordon who looked horrified, studying her face.

"No no. I won't do that."

"Good girl," he was clearly relieved. "I didn't think you were one of those silly kiss and tell women. No point. Only upsets people for nothing. Have to know when to let go."

He obviously had it all worked out. Roz couldn't wait for him to go then. It was too easy, too much under his control. She didn't like the role she was suddenly playing. The easy conniving weekend dalliance, no strings attached, everything going on the same as before. She didn't feel the same as before. Just how well did Paula know her own husband?

He left, not noticing any difference in the final embrace. She closed the door and poured herself another drink, suddenly feeling rather grubby. There was no way she'd ever tell Bill, no way she wanted Paula to know. The only problem was whether or not she could carry on as before, as if nothing had happened. Was it true what they said about boring marriages needing affairs to enliven them? Did all marriages become boring? How could Paula be bored with Gordon?

She knew the answers. Somehow she would have to cope, not resort to another drink when she was teaching in the morning. She took several panadeine instead, trying to stop her mind from running on ahead of her as she lay in bed, struggling to sleep.

It's taken her several days to stop feeling dazed and

guilty. She's pleased when the week ends. Even Gareth has left her alone at rehearsals. Although Bill has rung to say he's staying on through to Sunday she doesn't go for a drink on Friday night.

When Gordon rings, having heard Bill is still away, she says no without hesitation to his suggestion of a second trip.

"You're probably right," Gordon doesn't sound too disappointed. "Better to leave it as it is, not go back."

She wonders if he'll find a substitute, if they'll go to the same 'discreet' lodge. She feels mildly angry on Paula's behalf. Men. Can't trust them. Would have served Bill right... No, she's made her choice. She mentally plans a self indulgent solo weekend, with the place to herself. She'll even find time to write to Paula. It'll be easy, a bit of retrospective on Australia with Emma, details of the play rehearsals with a joke about Gareth. That'll fill several pages. Life is back in proportion again. Funny how it doesn't feel lonely any more.

Chapter Fifteen

Eleanor is first down in the morning, the scents of coffee and even grilled ham rising to wake Paula.

"Is he coming down?" Paula asks sleepily.

"Yes. He'll be down," there are steps on the stairs as Eleanor speaks. Paula catches an amused exchange of glances between Eleanor and the man who comes into the room. She is initially surprised that Robert is so much older than the other friends she's met. Then she realises how much he looks like Alain Delon, in a film they saw just last week. Robert is greyer than Delon has yet admitted to being, but otherwise the resemblance is remarkable. Yes. Paula looks at Eleanor with surprised recognition.

"No. He's not even related. Robert Duruel, my friend Paula."

He kisses Paula's hand, then embraces Eleanor on both cheeks several times. Gallic charm evident, Paula blown away satisfactorily.

"You are finding the cottage agreeable? A nice holiday?" he asks Paula and she responds enthusiastically. Eleanor serves up hot milk and coffee while Paula butters a roll.

"Whose are the paintings? Yours?"

"No no. Eleanor's."

"Ah. I should have guessed. You would not show me last time you painted. These are good. You must continue."

"It's only to pass the time. You're the artist."

"Not really. My camera is a better instrument than my brush will ever be. I must show you my pictures of Africa, before I send them away."

"To *Life*?"

"And also the *National Geographic.* Two assignments. That must not overlap, so I have to choose carefully."

"You're working today?"

"Yes I must. You have looked at the dark room?"

"No. It's still locked."

"I didn't know there was one," Paula's surprised.

"Oh it's not inside. It's part of that barn where I left my car last night."

"That's why we didn't see it," Paula's still in detective mode, to Eleanor's amusement.

"We'll leave you to it then. Time we did some shopping, and it's market day this morning," Eleanor clears the plates.

"Don't get too much food. I am taking you both out tonight."

"We'll bring back some lunch at least. Give you a break."

"That would be lovely." He vanishes upstairs again, then comes down with a box case to take out to the barn.

"He's marvellous," Paula is wide eyed.

"Well," Eleanor shrugs, secretly proud. "He is rather special."

"I thought those others were so smooth and sophisticated, but he's beyond all that isn't he?"

"Yes, he's absolutely himself. Confident and established. The others are still trying."

"How long have you known him?"

"About ten years. He photographed me when I first worked in Paris. A group of us were asked to pose for a series of pictures."

"You were in a magazine then?"

"Yes. *Elle.* No big deal, but quite fun at the time."

"Have you got it? I want to see it."

"Not here, unless Robert's kept one."

"I'll ask him," Paula won't let it go.

"Come on. To market."

Eleanor is more silent than usual as they drive in to

Concarneau and wander around the crowded market. Paula exclaims at the leather ware again, indulging in a soft lamb skin bag. Last time it was a belt pouch. Eleanor teases her as they sit outside the hotel bar by the square, watching everyone else still milling around the stalls.

"You can't get things like this at home. I should get wallets for Gordon and Simon too, and a bag for Emma."

"Plenty of time. You can post stuff home some time. They'll all be here again next week."

"It's amazing. I suppose they travel round from market to market."

"A lot of them. The neighbouring towns have markets on different days. It's in Quimper tomorrow."

"Might Robert want to go?"

"I shouldn't think so. Expect he'll still be busy."

They go to the fish market after their coffee. Eleanor chooses fresh langoustines and medallion like cod cheeks to cook fresh for lunch. It's nearly one when they get back to the house. Robert is sitting out on the deck. He immediately pours some cooled muscadet and helps Eleanor prepare the food. Paula watches their easy camaraderie in the kitchen and knows she isn't needed. She thumbs through some magazines, taking them on to the deck in the sun. Eleanor brings out a checked cloth and leaves her to set the table outside.

Paula watches Eleanor closely through the meal, assessing the importance of Robert. Eleanor is blooming in his presence, opening up and relaxing in a way she has not done with her other friends. He's obviously different. She hasn't seen Eleanor look so calm, so happy, the whole time she's been with her. The hard cynical edge has vanished in the company of this man. For that Paula can love him. She knows there will be many more reasons to appreciate a man who can do this for Eleanor. She asks a question and Eleanor obviously doesn't hear, she's so lost in her thoughts.

"Dreaming again," Robert speaks softly, gently taking

Eleanor's hand.

"Not important. I was only offering to make the coffee."

"Thanks Polly," they let her go for a moment. She leaves Eleanor to sit near the trees with Robert, basking in his presence. As she goes she hears Robert's anxious question, then from the kitchen their voices float up. She hears without meaning to, not thinking about what they're saying.

"You look tired. You're not...?"

"No no. A late night, that's all."

"Do you think you could come away with me? Take these photos to Paris then have a few days somewhere?"

"Yes please."

"It would be simple? Paula would not mind?"

"I think she'll fit in, for you."

"Why for me?"

"She already knows you're special."

"She has not made you regret the family you did not have?"

"How could I now?"

"Most people like to leave a replica, their name perhaps."

"Not me. You know that. Not the natural mother at all. How's your Daniel?"

Robert is happily talking about his son, who manages a gallery in Paris, and whose sculptures are finding some acclaim, when Paula brings the coffee. The lazy afternoon only finishes when Robert realises the time, going back to his dark room. Eleanor looks after him with longing eyes. Paula realises she is staying for her, instead of going to help him, but she says nothing. What can she say?

"Let's go for a walk to the beach," Eleanor is restless. They fetch hats and put on trainers to walk. When they reach the coast Eleanor tells Paula that Robert has asked her to go away with him for a while.

"Sure. I'm not surprised you know." Paula is agreeable.

"You won't mind being on your own?"

"I think I won't stay out here."

"You could have the car."

"Oh no. I haven't driven on the right. But it's OK. I'd like to stay in the heart of town for a while. A hotel in Concarneau."

"If you think you'd be happier. There's a good bus service to Quimper and lots of other places. You can go back to Pont Aven, or Bénodet."

"I'd like to do that river trip from Quimper to Bénodet. Maybe I'll spend a night or two in both places."

"You know Rémy and Anne-Marie will be pleased to have you again. I'll give them a call."

"Don't bother. Just leave me the number in case."

They sit on the wild beach. Eleanor seems lost in thought again, perhaps dreaming of driving off with Robert. Even Paula is silent, in her own thoughts and plans. Perhaps it's time they had a bit of a break from each other. It's already well into June.

Dear Roz,

Great to get your letter. The play sounds really good, but I don't believe that Gareth is behaving himself as well as you seem to imply!

I'm delighted you had Emma with you in Sydney. Thanks a lot, her letters have been full of enthusiasm. Hope it really wasn't too much of an imposition. You're welcome to have a daughter any time you like. She's even told me I can stay away for the August holidays if she can do something with you again! Doubt if Simon would miss me either, he's so full of all his exchanges with friends. Thanks for offering to have one of his friends home with your boys for midterm.

Hard to believe June's nearly gone. I'm now in a hotel in Concarneau, right in the the centre by the big market square and the bridge to the 'ville close', opposite the port and fish market. Super old building of four floors and then attics. Robert, the friend of Eleanor's who owns the house, showed me some photos of the same hotel around the turn of the century, with horses and old sailing fishing boats in a kind of basin where the market square is now, with an entrance from the river. Fascinating. He even told me where to go to a photographer in town to get copies of photos and postcards of that period.

I've been reading up all the local history and legends, wonderful place. Anyway I'm in town because Eleanor has driven off with Robert to take his African photos to Paris and have a bit of a break with him. Presumably before he vanishes on some other assignment. I could see they were really close, and it's actually nice to have some time to myself. Eleanor offered me her car, and of course the house, but you know me, I'm not game to drive on the right hand side of the road, my reflexes would go haywire.

It's so good to be in the heart of town. My room on the second floor has a view of the 'ville close,' the market, everything. I see the French house wives buying their bread and vegetables and seafood, fresh every day. I get 'carottes rapées' (no, it's grated, not raped) from the charcutier in the covered market, he sees me coming, and fresh fruit in the small daily market. The big market is on Friday and you can buy just about anything, honey, cheeses, wood and china ware, clothing, leather, old and new books (my downfall of course) and all sorts of rubbish or rare finds, according to what you want. I spend all that morning wandering around in the crush, loving it. The local library is good too, with a great reading room where I write and do research into all their literary magazines and history books. There's a research laboratory of Marine Biology on the corniche by the river mouth with a good museum, and the library is full of marine and shipping books. Hope I'm still here for their annual Salon of Maritime Books and then the Fête des Filets Bleus for the fishermen.

I go to films too, the cinema centre has three different films at a time, with one night a week for 'version originale' of foreign films (usually English) with French subtitles. Great.

So time is passing very pleasantly. It's the summer solstice in a couple of days and here it's a music festival, with all the different kinds of music in various parts of the town. I've even heard singers with little keyboards or guitars practising in the streets, and there'll be a classical concert in one place, a rock concert in the open space behind the ramparts at the end of the 'ville close'. I've discovered that the traditional jazz will be in the Place de la Mairie, just around the corner from the market in the big enclosed square by the library. So that's where I'll be going for my 'midsummer madness'. Pity they don't have anything like that at home. I think the English go a bit mad then too. Such a nice idea.

Hope the play goes off well. I'm sure you'll be superb. Wish everyone luck from me. And enjoy, even if Gareth is being boring! I shall raise a glass to you all.

Love,
Paula.

Paula's pleased to finally hear from Roz with a long newsy letter. The weather suddenly becomes much warmer in June, and with the beach just a couple of blocks away Paula swims at high tide most days, having light picnic lunches on the sand, or going into the pleasant new crêperie opposite the promenade. Sometimes she walks right around to the furthest beach, named after its white sands, with its tourist hotels and a friendly local bar right in the middle of them, above the bay. She sits on the terrace there to write, when she isn't watching the people on the beach, the boats, the whole vista. Her ordinary life has become so remote as time passes, even the letters seem to be from another world, not really bringing it closer at all. Her family are managing very well without her, she doesn't feel particularly missed, or needed. She's thriving on the luxury of time alone, time entirely for herself, for probably the first time in her life.

Then it's the evening of the solstice, midsummer night's eve. She eats early on the verandah of a pleasant restaurant in the ville close. She usually avoids such tourist crowded places in favour of the back street restaurants filled with locals, generally both cheaper and better. But she feels like being part of the moving scene this evening, joining the crowds, hearing the Breton bagpipes played as she walks through the gate, the local flutes on the corner near where she sits. It's a warm balmy evening, the light stretching on until late, the sun still quite high as she strolls back into town and up to the square by the Mairie. Already the outside tables of the only café, near the library, are filled, the jazz musicians are setting up.

Paula watches for a while, then a man who has smiled at her in the bookshop by the square where she buys a paper each day, catches her eye, gesturing to an empty chair at his table of cheerful laughing people. She sits down gratefully, soon absorbed in their friendliness, the whole open spirit of the evening.

Sipping muscadet, chatting, listening to the jazz warming up and taking off as the crowd increases, forming a semi circle around the musicians, Paula finds the whole scene irresistible. She always did have an urge to move when listening to jazz. Her feet tap in time before Bertrand nods to the open patch and stands up.

She doesn't hesitate, even though the space is empty. Rising naturally she just moves to the music as it takes her. Shades of drama parties, letting herself go, not caring what she looks like, enjoying the anonymity. Everyone laughs and encourages them both, and soon others join in, sharing the whole festival mood.

They pause to sip their drinks with the musicians, laughing at each other's antics. Then she catches an eye above her glass, across the other side. It's Jean-Pierre.

She thought they were long gone back to Paris.

He comes around to join her, introducing the man with him as his brother, Julien.

Paula looks at Julien and her eyes are held by the shrewd blue of his. Fisherman's eyes? The same Breton Celtic features as Jean-Pierre, but taller, with more presence. More electricity, she's forced to admit to herself almost immediately, as without preliminaries he sweeps her into the dance again.

Jean-Pierre finds his own partner. As she twirls she sees Catherine and Claude wandering up from the road, joining languidly in the moving mass.

It all goes on forever, suspended in time, the moon coming up, the warm darkness falling, the mood becoming even more exuberant and noisy as the midnight hour passes.

The vortex of whirling shapes finally tosses her to one side, breathless, clinging to this solid stranger. The others join them.

"We went out to the house to find you. It's all closed. What's happened?" Claude greets her with an affectionate hug.

She explains.

"I've got a key though if you want to stay there," she hastens to inform them, being sure that would normally happen.

"Come out with us. We can all stay there," Julien holds her arm, reinforcing the invitation with those eyes, deep as the sea.

"No thanks. I'm too tired to do more than walk to the

hotel," she digs in her belt pouch, fastened on before coming out to leave her hands free, finds the key and hands it to Claude.

Suddenly her head spins, she knows she's had enough, enough dancing, enough drinking, enough people. She can't cope with any more, pleased that the hotel is so close. They walk with her, silently. She's glad of a supporting arm.

"We're driving back to Paris in the morning. We've already stayed away too long." They pause at the door of the hotel, Claude looking at her.

"Can we drop the key in to you on the way?"

"Sure. You can leave it at the desk if I'm not down."

"Afraid we will have to leave quite early," Catherine gives her a warm hug. "You look after yourself. Come to me in Paris if you get bored and Eleanor's not back," she gives Paula her address card, with the phone number on it.

She lets the men embrace her farewell in a daze, then slips up to her room, falling into bed, still floating with the excitement, the heady encounter, the throb of the music, mercifully too faint to keep her awake once the shutters are closed.

She wakes late and stretches lazily, mentally planning a leisurely day. When she finally opens the shutters it's grey, with a misty rain falling. She goes down to coffee and croissants in the hotel's corner bar, where on fine days tourists fill the strip of tables and chairs on the pavement stretching along the main road, and around the corner by the market. Today the door is closed, and each entry brings the removal of a damp coat, the closing of a dripping umbrella, before it swings shut again.

She stays by the window, gazing out over a second coffee, wondering what to do. Perhaps a walk through the covered market and then to the library. It looks just the right sort of day to finish following the references to Jean Giono she found in the literary magazines there, photocopying pages into vast piles of reference material she really must post home some time. In between she has been reading several of his books, one a boxed gem she found at the market stall, 'Le Déserteur', with its engravings and poignant depiction of the traces of a real life.

She fetches her coat and small folding umbrella. The man in the bookshop waves as she passes, her charcutier looks up in the market, but his usual queue waits and she goes on to buy some fruit, fascinated as always by the way similar stalls will be one with a long queue, another with no-one. Indications of the French discrimination in food, Eleanor says. Follow the queues to the best stalls.

Tucking the apple and pear in her shoulder bag she goes out the back door of the market, pausing to raise her umbrella blindly, against a sudden gust behind the building. A man's laugh startles her, the deep broken voice awakening recognition before she raises the umbrella and sees Julien.

"You nearly got me," he's still laughing.

"I thought you'd gone back to Paris with the others."

"No. What made you think that? I haven't become a Parisien like Jean-Pierre."

"Guess I didn't really think," she's pleased to see him.

"I'm getting wet. That little thing of yours is useless," she is trying to include him in its shelter. "Let's have a coffee."

They run laughing to the nearest café, the library forgotten.

"Do you live here then?"

"No. My mother is at Audierne, so I have a room there, or at Jean-Pierre's in Paris. My own place is a cottage in Ireland, on a hill above Bantry Bay."

"Ireland? How marvellous. What do you do? Do you spend much time there?"

"Not enough. I travel in fish, seafood. Boring really. But Ireland and Brittany are important sources. I arrange shipments, find markets, travel around Europe."

"That doesn't sound boring."

"Believe me. Too much on the road, no roots. Plays havoc with normal life."

"You have a family?"

"Did have. Not a job that's fair to families. My wife found a better man. Now everyone's happy."

"Do you see much of your children?"

"Enough. They have their own lives to live. They don't want to end up a bum like me."

"You were always travelling?" she wonders if his wife knew when they married. He follows her thoughts.

"No. I was at sea first, doing the fishing. She always wanted me to have a land job, be safer, so I did." There's no bitterness in his voice. So she was right about the fisherman's eyes.

They talk on about children, Brittany, Ireland. Paula tells him the Miss Gray story, communicating to him all her excitement about it. He responds eagerly, offering to drive her back to Bénodet when it's time to check out the photographs. The morning passes so easily it's a while before they notice the rain has stopped and a weak sun is becoming stronger, warming the steaming pavement outside.

"Now we can go to lunch," he announces with satisfaction.

"What about your work?"

"Nearly finished here. One call to make this afternoon and that's it."

"So you'll be gone," she's disappointed.

"One last night at my mother's. Come with me. You'll like her, and there are some pretty walks around Audierne."

"It's on a river mouth too isn't it?"

"Yes. Further west. You've been there?"

"No. I've just seen it on the map. I'd love to visit Audierne, meet your mother."

"You shall. Now we're going to drive away from town to eat, a leisurely lunch in the country."

"Would you mind stopping at the Post Office? I haven't collected my mail for a couple of days." They pick up his Range Rover in the square and drive past the hotel. She can't help feeling how suitable the vehicle is. He pauses outside the Post Office and she comes out waving an envelope from Bénodet, as well as the usual from her family.

"I'll look at them later," she tucks them in her bag.

It's the same restaurant she has been to with the others, including his brother. Perhaps a family favourite. She doesn't say anything, letting him think that all the pleasures to which he is introducing her are absolutely new. They feel new anyway with him, she can't even remember what she ate last time. She expresses delight at the antique Breton dolls on the high shelves above the tables, dressed in the costumes and coiffes of the region. She likes the atmosphere, the old wood panelled walls, the fine linen. The patron gives her a discreet wink, not letting on that he's seen her before.

It's much later, the meal finished as they sit on over coffee, when she remembers her mail. He has left her for a moment, and she pulls it all out, opening the Bénodet note first as the most exciting. When he returns she can't wait to tell him.

"They've found a photo," he smiles as she bubbles on. "They want me to come and see them."

"Did they find his name?"

"Yes, but not on the photo. Her daughter found a forgotten old visitor's book in the attic with all their albums. They had both signed it."

"So what's his name?"

"William Grogan."

"Ah. There are so many Grogans in Ireland."

"Guess it's hopeless then."

"Not necessarily. Where was he from?"

"Castletownbere."

"That's on Bantry Bay too. It could be well worth a try. You'd only need to ask around the bars, the locals would know."

"You might recognise him from the photos."

"That's possible."

"Don't suppose I'll ever know now."

"I've been thinking," Julien reaches across the table to where her hand is lying on the white cloth, touching her fingers, entwining them with his own. "You must come to Ireland with me. You would love it."

"Now?" Paula is startled.

"Yes. Why not?"

"But your work?"

"That's where I'm going, imbécile. I'm due there by the end of the week." His use of the word Robert used to Eleanor seems to seal something. Said in French it's not an insult, more an affectionate pet name.

Paula gazes at him, her dawning delight evident. Why not indeed?

Suddenly the future opens up in all directions, almost too quickly. Should she go? She certainly wants to. There's nothing really to stop her. She can follow the Miss Gray trail to Ireland, and not least, she can run away with this exciting man. No-one need know. Maybe it's all about following gut feelings, instincts. Rushing on like the water around the rock in the Taoist books she has read at Robert's. She looks into the calm expectant blue eyes opposite.

"I'd love to come to Ireland," the words are firm, confident. She's ready.

Everything happens so quickly that Paula feels stunned. Before they leave the restaurant Julien uses the phone and they're booked on the car ferry to Cork tomorrow night. While he makes his last business call she's at the hotel, packing her bag and checking out. Then they drive out to Robert's house to leave a note for Eleanor, along with Paula's excess luggage. The drive to Audierne is her first chance to really draw breath since making the decision. She feels good about it, safe with this big bear of a man. Eleanor knows him and his brother, of course it's all right.

They call at Bénodet on the way. Madame Guéguin is enchanted by Julien. She brings out a small faded photograph and they study it together. Miss Gray is not wearing glasses, her hair is loose and attractive, her eyes shine, her expression echoing that of the tall man holding her arm. Paula is thrilled. Julien looks at it closely, then shakes his head.

"It could be any one of several people I know," he says. "It's just not clear enough to be sure."

They pause for an apéritif, Julien chatting to the French woman with his easy charm.

If she still has any doubts his mother allays them. This comfortable dumpling of a strong capable Bretonne, who Julien assures her still wears the coiffe on Sundays and for the annual Pardon, is kindness personified. She embraces Paula and bustles around showing her to a room filled by a huge bed swamped in a billowing feather duvet. Then she sits her down for a drink with Julien while she prepares a delectable meal.

"You can see why I come home. No restaurant to match my mother's cooking," he's into his second helping of tarte tatin with generous dollops of cream. Paula feels as if she'll never be able to eat another mouthful.

She's not allowed to help clear up. She relaxes on the verandah looking down river as the sunset colours the water and the sea birds swoop in the tidal mud. Julien helps his mother and she can hear laughter in the kitchen. The warm affection between them is striking. They join her with coffee, and slices of the rich Breton butter cake, home made of course. She even finds room for a piece, thankful for the gap after dinner.

"Sleep well," Julien tells her as she goes off to bed, replete. "You mightn't sleep so well on the boat tomorrow night."

"Of course she will," his mother scolds him. "So big they are now, those ferries."

They make a leisurely start the next day. As they drive north Julien keeps stopping in quaint little towns, showing her beautiful old calvaries, steeples, even a ruined abbey and a chateau. He evidently loves his homeland, a proud Breton, describing the history of the region and the particular legends attached to each stopping place. Paula treasures it all. It's refreshing to hear his affection for the country after Eleanor's throw away rather cynical comments when they travel together.

She soon realises that the most wonderful thing about Julien is that he makes her laugh. Every little thing is amusing, her way of talking, his English, the food in Roscoff before they catch the ferry, the barman on the ferry where they have a last drink, before she goes off to the cabin she shares with three other women.

The voyage becomes even more enchanting when they reach Ireland. Their first stop is a pub in Cork where she throws a coin in a fountain to make sure she will return to Ireland one day. Then they drive across the county to the south west corner and his cottage on the hill above the bay. A mystical mountain retreat, surrounded by trees, bush, rearing rocks, overlooking the water through the branches, past the island with the Italian gardens and the rock where Julien shows her the seals basking through his binoculars.

It's magic. The laughter, the dawning relationship that blows her away more quickly than she admits, the whole sense of release and escape from reality. Time out of life. The most bizarre thing about it, and probably the most Irish, is that she's in Ireland speaking French practically all the time, from choice because its musical sounds seem to fit the place, the man, the feelings.

The first night they eat in a local pub, and walk up the long hill afterwards. As she stumbles on the uneven track he takes her hand, holding it lightly for the rest of their walk. She realises the pulses of his warm fingers are making her tremble all over with suppressed excitement. At first she thinks it is just a friendly gesture, then as they reach the cottage he pauses for a moment, turning her around to look at the view, the moonlight on the bay below them. He is silent, but his eyes are seeking hers with a question in them, and suddenly it's impossible to resist the urge to respond, to take his other hand as he offers it, then to let his arms go around her in a hug that lifts her into the air, almost kicking her legs in pleasure. There is still a moment of choice when they go inside, but by then Paula is so immersed in sensual indulgence that she barely notices it. What seems like a dream becomes so urgently physical she is gasping outside her mind almost before they reach the bed.

It is not until the next morning, waking with her head on his chest, feeling the lazy stir of his arms around her, that Paula realises the cottage has only one bedroom, where Julien put her bag when they arrived. She grins to herself at the thought that he would have had to sleep on the narrow settle in the living room if passion had not carried her away.

As the days pass they drive around, take boat rides, explore mountains, lakes and peat bogs. Paula knows she will never be able to tell anyone all about this visit. When he drives off at times to do business, she walks the hills and shores, or sits beneath the trees dreaming, her gaze on the water. He picks her wild cotton, blazing fuchsias line the long rough drive way up the hill to his place, an old wooden croft where they play at house together. She's charmed, enchanted, even to the extent of forgetting all about Miss Gray for several days.

They chat with a number of locals in the village, share meals a couple of times, once with a French couple Julien knows, another time an Englishman married to a beautiful Irish woman. Julien is at home with everyone, talking to barmen, finding the best places to eat when they drive into Bantry, giving her a continual amusing commentary on all their trips. He pokes fun at her New Zealandness and the contrasts between New Zealand and France, often in her favour, not his, making her laugh and loosen up so completely she wonders how she can ever stop. 'Complicité' he calls it, as they share so much she knows life will never seem the same again.

Then back to reality, her search reminding her of all she has so resolutely cut out of her mind. The slow realisation that however earth shattering this particular explosion it's not her life, will have to end. When it's over her Frenchman, his echoing voice, mannerisms, touch, above all his laughter, will resonate in her brain forever while he rides off into the Irish mists and bogs, the European trade routes, his own haunting future. For he is haunted. The particular combination of Irish fey and Breton Celtic mysticism really does make him impossible to pin down, a natural wanderer. When she discovers this, she tries to protect herself, her feelings, a little, even as he is already trying to protect her, save her from giving too much of herself to what they both know cannot last. They manage to laugh at each other in this as well, making a joke of it all, the ships in the night of romantic cliché, the knight riding off to the crusades, wearing his lady's favour. She gives him her red silk scarf on the spot, watching him wrap it around his neck smugly. Soon he will vanish into his own future, and she will never know where he is, what he's doing, even if he still lives. How will she bear it?

Each time Julien chats with locals over a drink he asks about the name Grogan, gathering and rejecting information as the week passes. Finally they find time to drive out to the Ring of Beara and Castletownbere, to ask specifically in the pubs there. He brings her drink over to the table in an old bar overlooking a grassy knoll that ends in a small mooring place for fishing boats. The hills behind the road are typically bare, with large rocks jutting at intervals. This time he's been lucky. There is a William Grogan, quite old now, but gone to Dublin to his sister's to live. The Irishman who told Julien follows him outside to join them.

"You could be calling on his daughter," he says, putting his glass of guinness on the table.

"He has a daughter?"

"Yes. About twenty five she is. Got a wee son herself,

but the father was drowned in a boating accident. They lived with William until he left." Paddy has settled to yarn with them, ready to tell all he can. Paula is hopeful, this is her best chance. Is it the right one?

"Tell me about him. He was married then?"

"Yes. It was one of those marriages made in dreams. But she had the tuberculosis. He had to put her in a clinic for long periods of time."

"How sad."

"She would be all right for while, then it would rear again."

"How did he cope?"

"His sister moved in. When the baby came home with her the sister stayed and looked after them all."

"His wife's still alive?"

"No. She died about ten years ago. She'd been less and less at home, he'd taken to travelling a lot, escaping his own demons."

"And the poor child?"

"Not really. She's lovely. An independent young woman, strong in her own way."

"Tragic about her husband."

"Well, they weren't married. It was before she had the child and she's done really well."

"If she's twenty five, you think her mother had her in the clinic?"

"Of course. They came back together."

Julien goes into the bar for another round, Paddy's glass is empty. Paula's mind races with startling thoughts. But she can't be right. Miss Gray would never have left a daughter. She doesn't even know if it's the right William.

"We could call on her," Paddy raises his brimming glass, including himself in the quest now.

"Would she mind?" Paula is doubtful but Julien leaps on the idea.

"Shouldn't we ring first?"

"She won't have the telephone," Paddy's glass is empty again and he rises to show them the way. As he goes into the bar first to get his jacket, Paula turns to Julien.

"Do you think it's him?"

"Could be. Do you think your Miss Gray came here?"

"I'm sure she did, those paintings Madame Guéguin talked about, the stones on the hills."

They drive around the bay to a house the other side of the village in the long evening. Paula has got so used to them the shorter twilights at home will be strange.

Siobhan Grogan is lovely. Long black hair, smooth white skin, a laughing lilt to her husky voice. The wee boy at her feet, little William, after her father, is a cheerful elfin child, shyly showing the lady with a funny voice his chunkily hewn wooden toys.

"Father made him his toys," Siobhan is proud, indicating a whole box full, trucks with wheels, animals and building blocks. Little William tips them all out for her with a gleeful chuckle.

"Wicked child," his mother lovingly scoops him up for a cuddle, then sets him down in the middle of them while she pours the visitors drinks.

"You're over often?" she gives Julien a whisky. She's already questioned him closely about what brings him to Ireland.

"Quite often. I've spent a lot of time in Spain recently."

"I thought the French fishermen were fighting with the Spanish fishermen."

"Ah but the Germans still want their fish."

"So you drive around arranging it all."

"It gives me a living."

"You haven't bought a plane yet?"

"That would be nice, but it's still a dream."

Paula follows the conversation with interest, learning more about this man who doesn't talk much about himself.

"And your father then," says Paddy. "He's after coming back soon?"

"Oh he's settled now. But he'll visit for Willy's

155

birthday. Otherwise it'll be us that travel to see him for Christmas."

"So when's the big day?" Julien looks at the boy.

"This Saturday. Would you like to come? Just a few friends, he won't know what it's about." She looks fondly at her son, who's knocking over his tower of building blocks.

"Is your son very much like him?" Paula's question is tentative.

"He has the eyes. Would you be wanting to see a photograph then, you can see for yourself."

Paula can't believe her luck. Siobhan pulls out a box and thumbs through a stack of photographs, passing her several of young William at various stages. She makes appreciative noises, almost holding her breath. Then there's a photo of the two of them, young William on his grandfather's knee, laughing together. She feels there's no mistaking it. It's the man in the photograph with Miss Gray. She hands it to Julien for confirmation.

"I think it's the same man. You're right," he looks again, then Paddy takes it.

"Old Bill and little Willy," he says. "The little one will be missing him."

It is Julien who explains to Siobhan how Paula is following the footsteps of her employer, a woman who painted in Brittany and Ireland, but the mention of her name brings no response from Siobhan so they let it slip by. When the wee boy becomes restless they leave in search of a meal in the local hotel. Siobhan assures them of a welcome on Saturday and they promise to return. As they eat the fresh Irish salmon, the local mussels, the only Irish food worth eating according to her Frenchman, Paula dares hope that the solution to her quest is in sight. Julien tells her she's fortunate, they have to take the Saturday night ferry back to Brittany, so William is coming just in time. Paula has a moment of shock that the end is so close, then the anticipation takes over again and she can hardly wait for Saturday. Paddy has joined them for a meal, chatting with Julien about fishing, then heading off into another bar when they leave to drive back to Julien's cottage.

When the time comes Paula feels a bit nervous. Should she be doing this? Siobhan's small house is filled with children, smiling Irish women work in the tiny kitchen and men sit outside with their guinness, yarning as they look across the bay. They will have to leave early to drive to Cork for the ferry. Which one is William?

They give their gift to the young boy running around with his friends. Paula has carefully chosen several books from a shop in Bantry, delighted to find one by New Zealander Margaret Mahy. Young William expresses delight, then puts the books on the heap of presents by the fireplace and runs off with his friends. Siobhan makes sure they have drinks before she takes them outside to meet her father. Paula hesitates.

The big man who greets them makes it easy. The beard is white now, but the green eyes haven't lost their keenness. She remembers the time she saw Miss Gray's eyes unveiled by her glasses. Green, similar. She can imagine these two pairs of eyes responding to each other, as in the photograph. As soon as she mentions Virginia Gray his eyes become misty pools of memory.

"How is she?" the immediate question holds all the warmth of real concern, and Paula answers as fully as she can.

"I tried to find her, nine or ten years ago. My letters came back undelivered."

"You know her travel book?" the question has hung in her mind, is he the companion?

"Oh yes. I still have it. It was our trip. I'd been in China, my one great voyage to fulfil a dream and to find a Chinese cure for my Maureen. Those traditional herbal cures, they work miracles sometimes, the ancient wisdoms." He remembers again, and she knows how much he loved his wife, his pilgrimage for her. There was evidently no miracle.

"It was cheaper by train, though it took so long.

157

Virginie" the French pronunciation again, "was on the same trip. It was something rather special to share together."

"I've read the book. It sounded the trip of a lifetime."

"It was, it was. Did the book go well in New Zealand?"

"I don't think she ever released it there. I only saw her copy. She didn't think people would be interested."

"Too modest. Always too modest. I told her."

He chases his guinness with a whiskey in the local fashion. They are sitting on the garden wall now, away from the others. Someone brings them a plate of salmon sandwiches. Julien stays silent, following their discussion, William's memories. Paula dreams wildly of bringing them together, her Miss Gray and this gentle giant. And Siobhan? How can she ask? Is it any of her business?

"We shared a lot of time in France. She was a good painter. Did she continue?"

"No. Not at all. I didn't even know she painted till I met someone she knew."

"Poor little Virginie. Her few years of courage. Did she really let it all go?"

"Yes. I don't know why."

"It was the baby, the treatment." He's no longer talking to her. It's a private memory, that nobody can stop or interrupt. "Maureen was so bad when I went, she hadn't been able to leave the clinic for nearly a year. It was a last desperate chance. The treatment seemed to help a little. She came home for short periods, but each winter she would have to go back. Then there seemed to be a real remission. Virginie came here with me, looked after Maureen at home one late summer. We watched her bloom again. It was my miracle. Virginie left to paint in the south of France, to finish the proofs of the travel book. It was perhaps the pregnancy that was unwise, but Maureen wanted so much to have a child and I couldn't deny her anything. It brought it on again, she had to go to the clinic to have Siobhan. My sister came to care for us, she was newly widowed. Virginie came back with the book for me, saw how it was, how the time would be with the child, with Maureen so fragile, and she left. She gave up all she had made this side of the world and went back to New Zealand. She only ever sent postcards, Christmas cards. She didn't answer my letters. I didn't understand why."

He eats his sandwich without seeing it. Paula can see that he really hasn't understood, that he still doesn't know how Virginie could have left. He seems not to be able to comprehend that he must have been the love of her life, and she made the supreme sacrifice for the sake of his wife and child. Then when his wife died and he tried to get in touch again, Miss Gray must have known, must have chosen, decided it was too late, perhaps not even opened the letters.

Paula knows she has meddled in the closed book of someone's life. She cannot interfere with decisions that were made, so many years before. Was it a matter of money? William obviously lives simply, his one big trip by train to China. Miss Gray lives modestly, her old car, the bookshop that probably doesn't make more than a small living. They met on their single adventures of a lifetime, and although they spun out the meetings over several years, it still ended, just as her week with Julien is ending. The poignancy, the sentimental clutch at her throat, is only an echo through time. Nothing changes. For some people there can only ever be a brief connection between vastly different worlds. She could not live in Ireland, or even France. She would only ever be a visitor. Miss Gray must have made the same decision, chosen not to stay. And she was wrong about the child, the little romantic dream that perhaps Miss Gray had even given up her baby. All just a fantasy.

The noise of the party, the cries of happy children, intrude on the silence of their thoughts, private thoughts for each, as he remembers, she bites her lip to still the tumble of words and Julien watches them both. Julien fetches more drinks. The garden with its worn grass and border of fuchsias becomes visible again as the mists of mind clear. William shakes his leonine head and starts asking Julien questions about his travels. The world settles into normality again, salmon sandwiches and guinness and old men sitting on wooden benches in the sun. There's nothing more to say, even to Julien.

Chapter Sixteen

Dear Nell,
You didn't tell me Jean-Pierre had a brother.
Will you be astonished to know that I am here
in Ireland with him? I suspect nothing will
startle you, but it did me. Herself surprised,
caught in shock, carried off, willingly I assure
you. Blame the midsummer madness, the music
fest in Concarneau where we met.
Isn't Ireland an amazing place? Magic, mystic,
so beautiful it is another home coming. I can
see why people speak of it with far away looks
in their eyes. It has captured me too, claimed
a piece of my heart forever.
We met with William Grogan's daughter today,
and hopefully with him soon. At least I'm pretty
sure it's him, the photos seem to match. It no
longer feels so urgent now I am sure that Miss
Gray once shared this ambience, must some
time have been equally enchanted by France
and Ireland both, the Celtic mists and echoes.
Maybe I don't need to know details that may
haunt me, the place obsesses me enough.
Perhaps I'll even break out in poetry.
If this letter and you meet before my return just
smile for me, pal. I hope your travels have been
as rewarding.
Love from Polly.

Eleanor reads Paula's letter with her amused smile.
Trust Polly. Of course she's having a wonderful time
with Julien. She wonders about her own motives for not
mentioning him to Polly. Is it the fact that, so different

161

from his brother, he's a special part of her own past? She chuckles, remembering the teddy bear he gave her, a substitute for his absences. No she's not jealous. Not in the least. Both she and Julien have moved on. Robert is far closer to her than Julien ever was.

Dear Robert. They've been having such a super time together. She's revelling in having him to herself at last. Feeling fulfilled in a way she has only ever done during their fleeting connections in the past. He's her taste of real life, real achievement. He makes her feel that without him she only plays at living. Her whole life has become a performance of sorts, waiting in the wings until he comes along to make her realise who she really is. Through the years she has found herself waiting expectantly for his returns, his exotic glimpses of other worlds, his stories, but above all the sheer peace of being with him, of sharing everything, getting her life in proportion again. He has finally begun to talk of stopping, maybe settling in just one or two different places to chase the seasons, and it's too late.

Now they're back in Brittany she asks him about his next assignment, steeling herself for his departure. He gives her a pleasant surprise.

"I'm not going on one. I turned it down to come back early."

"Why? You're all right?" she's suddenly anxious.

"Of course. I just thought we needed this time together, you and me."

"You must have felt my own feeling."

"Naturally. But I came to see if you might prefer just to be with your childhood friend. If so I would have gone away."

"And you found us ready to have a bit of space."

"Fortuitous. And you freed her to go off with Julien."

"Not specifically," they laugh. She has read him Paula's letter, shared the news when there was no sign of her at the hotel. "I'm pleased she's having her fling with Julien. He's kind."

"You don't mind?"

162

"Of course not. I have you."

"We have each other," the normally unsentimental Robert allows his eyes to soften. Their complicity is complete. Two practical hard headed quite cynical people, with their own problems, but an understanding of each other that goes beyond the ordinary. Right from the start. It's not the pity that it might have been that they did not get together more permanently. They both know it wouldn't have worked, that neither is made to be tied down, that the inevitable coming together in need will happen regardless. It always has.

"Will Paula go back to her marriage, that boring domestic life you described?"

"I'm hoping that her horizons will open up sufficiently to allow her to become something other than that. She always had the potential."

"She chose so differently from you."

"She was a different person. It was right for her then to seek that security."

"But not now?"

"I think she's grown out of it. Ready for something else."

"You don't think she might get too carried away with Julien, suffer too much when he moves on?"

"Bound to. The first time. I would have thought it too dangerous to ever set up."

"It happened without you."

"I'm sure she'll cope."

"We'll be here for her."

They are in the kitchen, companionably preparing food. It's a pleasure to Eleanor, cooking with someone as accomplished and food loving as Robert. It's the only time in her life she has enjoyed working in the kitchen, even if her contribution is mostly in the preparation, always laughingly directed by the 'chef' as she calls him. She's even tried some of the actual braising and baking, following his instructions. It's amazing to find that it's not so difficult after all if you know what you're doing and have the right ingredients. It's even a delight to go to the markets with him and carefully select the fruit and vegetables, the almost alive seafood. She doesn't want to do it on her own though, it's only worth doing with him.

"We may be misjudging Julien. Even he may be ready to stop." She remembers he did settle once, have a family.

"Can you see Paula staying in France, Europe?"

"No. Her children are too young, she still has the responsibility."

"That settles it. Julien would never leave."

"They will have realised already. They're not fools."

"Perhaps she will come back here one day."

"I may not be here," Eleanor catches his eyes and holds them in rare urgency.

"You must tell her," he's gentle.

"I was waiting till later. Not too soon."

"I think she will understand."

Robert lifts the pan from the stove, the meal is ready. As usual they take it outside to eat. Just the two of them.

They do not have long to wait. Paula and Julien arrive on Sunday night from the ferry, after a day exploring part of the northern coast. Paula is glowing, spilling over with their travels, all her impressions and discoveries.

"Don't you just love Ireland? You must," she embraces them both with her arms and her enthusiasm.

"I knew it would get her," Julien is smug, smiling in the background.

"It was only Ireland then?" Eleanor is a little tart, wondering if Paula expects more of him.

"Julien is off to Germany and then to Spain," Paula raves on. "I'm going to go along for the ride, see a bit more of Europe. If you don't mind," she hastily queries Eleanor with anxious eyes.

"No, I don't mind. Robert's not leaving again yet."

"Great."

"I've told her it will mean a lot of travelling, with only little bits of time to look around."

"I love travelling. It will be so good to see two more countries."

"And your Irish mystery?"

"Yes, it's all solved. Rather sad really," and Paula immediately tells them all about William, Maureen, Siobhan, and how Miss Gray left.

"So you won't need to say anything when you get back," Eleanor is concerned for Miss Gray.

"No. Don't worry. I won't rush in..."

"No stomping the angels," they grin at each other, tuned in again, while the two Frenchmen look at them, puzzled. They don't explain.

"I found spirals in Ireland too," Paula is off on the next tack.

"Celtic," Julien joins in.

"That spiral I found in the market, William recognised it."

"André Breton wrote about the Celtic spiral, the perpetual movement searching for man's destiny, the Celtic convulsion." Robert knows his history, his poets.

"Is that where he got his idea that beauty had to be convulsive?" Eleanor knows hers, too.

"Or it wasn't beauty. It's all linked. He studied the Celts, the Bretons, it was part of him."

"Can I borrow your book, to read on the road?"

"Markale? Of course. Rather a large book though."

"And the André Breton collection please."

"You won't have much time to read," Julien is dismissive of poetry. "We've only got a couple of days here. Off to Frankfurt on Wednesday."

"You'll stop on the way?"

"I thought a night in Paris," Julien is airy.

"Will you be back in time for Bastille Day?" Robert pulls out the two books to give Paula.

"Yes. Just. I have to be here again mid July."

"That's only about two weeks away," Paula's trip now has a limit. She's already reconciled to taking what she can get, unquestioning. Eleanor can see that in the way she follows Julien's words so carefully. Paula is still talking about the local myths she has found in Robert's books and in the library at Concarneau. Eleanor watches her, wondering how long the glow brought on by Julien will last. She hasn't seen Paula in the flush of love for such a long time, it suits her. Who was it said that every woman is beautiful when she's in love? She can only hope that Paula won't fall too far and too hard when the time comes. She has no faith in Julien. Paula is still talking to Robert.

"After going to Ireland I'd like to get an overview of the Celts."

"Are your origins Celtic?" Robert is open to anyone with his own interests.

"I think there's some Scottish bits, a great grandfather from Edinburgh."

"Such an interesting mix of origins, New Zealand must be."

"It's all got a bit remote now, several generations on. Not so many people are keen to look up where they came from."

"That's as it should be. You are New Zealanders now. Do you have local blood too?"

"Yes. A great grandmother."

"So you know the language, the culture?"

"Not very well. I've stayed on a marae with distant cousins, studied one paper at university. I find when I try to use it with my friends I've forgotten most of it."

"They all speak English now?"

"Oh yes. There's a marvellous movement of language nests in the infant school though, to save the language."

"You didn't tell me about that," Eleanor knows Paula doesn't expect her to be interested. She thinks of a past boyfriend, how she used to watch him play rugby, then join him in performing the haka at the after match parties. She doesn't think he knew his own language, not many of their generation did. He used to sing and play the guitar, she remembers, super voice. She grins, remembering doing a high descant to the rugby team's shouted party songs, encouraging a shy Paula to join in. Then it was the cricket season and she fell for a visiting Australian bowler. She never was much good at continued allegiance.

"The French colonial attitude was very different. We did not try to assimilate other people as you did," Julien is a bit pompous.

"That only meant different problems, didn't it," Robert doesn't want to be sidetracked.

"Yes. Your record is not so hot either," Eleanor enjoys rubbing Julien up the wrong way. Scratch a patriot is one of her party games, in a country where everyone is so politically aware.

"We are talking about the New Zealand Maori and the Celts, not politics," Robert is firm.

"I think they have a lot in common actually."

"You mean the Celtic spiral and the Maori koru?" Eleanor follows Paula's thinking.

"Yes. It would be great to do a study of parallels, myths and art forms."

"There you are. Why don't you? A thesis topic for you."

"That's not silly."

"Go for it Polly."

"I could use the research I've done here, study this book for a start." Paula is full of the prospects. Eleanor knows she already has a stack of notes from Robert's books.

Robert tells her the writer may still be lecturing at the Sorbonne.

"That would be too much. Unreal."

"But not impossible."

"Impossible for the next few years anyway."

"Start it in Auckland, see where it takes you."

"I'd need to do more history papers first to qualify."

"Do them then."

Eleanor can see the awakening gleam of excitement in Paula's eyes. Robert is already pulling out other books that might interest her. His real collection is here, not in his small Paris apartment.

"It's late. My bedtime," Julien has had enough, and Paula soon follows him.

He's off on business the next morning. Paula spends the day in books, making notes, reading avidly. Robert answers her questions, sits in the garden with Eleanor. They walk along the coastal paths after lunch, then snooze in the orchard in the late heat of the afternoon. Julien finds them and scoffs at their apathy.

"There's a bee. You all need to be stung to wake you up," he cries, unnecessarily loud in the indolent haze.

"No thank you. I'm mildly allergic to them," Robert has not even opened his eyes. Julien drops petals on Paula's upturned face till she convulses with laughter and pounces on him, both tumbling in the grass.

"They make one feel quite old, don't they," Eleanor catches Robert's eye, laughing.

The next days pass quickly. Paula and Julien leave and they're back to just the two of them again. Eleanor enjoys the peace. It's so easy. Robert sorts out photographs, cataloguing, writing. She takes the paints out again, languid strokes of colour in the orchard, only bees droning in lethargy. She kids Robert into doing some more painting, watching awed as he dashes off stylish compositions with a sureness of brush and depth of paint that she can never begin to achieve. He spends time training her eye, her hand, to follow, until she gives way in laughter. A local gallery shows several pieces which sell easily at this height of the season. Cheerful postcards plot Paula's rapid travels across Europe until they finally return, just before Bastille day as promised. Eleanor is amused to see that Paula's luggage now includes a large soft teddy bear, almost the twin of her own.

"Guillaume," says Paula with a laugh when they have a moment alone.

"Not Julien?" Eleanor raises an eyebrow. Her own bear has no name. Just Bear.

Julien will move on straight after the fête, le quatorze juillet.

"You will still be here next time I pass?" they're back in the town square in the early evening, joining the crowds waiting for the local parade, the later firework display from the ramparts of the ville close.

"No. I'll be back home by then," Paula's very definite response surprises Eleanor.

"Where are you off to now?" Robert smoothly fills the silence.

"I'm going to the Mediterranean." It's obviously not news to Paula.

The parade, filled with small children in local costumes, starts. They join the crush to trail it around the market place. Music and dancing follow, later stilled at the impressive firework display, exploding from the old stone walls over the marina, the river, where illuminated boats move slowly.

"A super way to remember my stay here," Paula is still ecstatic as they return home, well into the hours of the next morning.

"But you're not leaving yet," Eleanor looks up.

"Soon. I've decided I'd like to be home in time for the August holidays after all." Eleanor saves her comments on that. She wants to talk to Paula without the men, or especially without Julien. She can wait.

"We'll miss you," Robert is a genuine host.

"I'll miss you too, everything here."

"You will have to come back then," Julien is definite. "Once you have been to Brittany, to Ireland, they will haunt you until you return."

"Yes. I know they will. But I've spent enough time here now."

"Naturally your family calls." Robert, the father, is the one who understands. Eleanor thinks fondly of his son, but she's glad she didn't know him as an infant, only as his own person, with his father's charm even in his early teens when she first met him. He has spent more time with his mother and her second husband, but his relationship with his father is still close. She stands up suddenly.

"If I don't go to bed soon I'll fall over. Apart from the fact that's it's nearly time to get up."

"We don't need to get up. Let's sleep in," and they follow her, sleepily.

Chapter Seventeen

Dear Roz,
You'll be wondering why you haven't heard for
so long. I've been travelling, and there's only
been time for quick cards to the family. I got this
chance to go to Ireland with some friends of
Eleanor's, and then they had business in
Germany and Spain so I spent a couple more
weeks travelling. Ireland was especially good,
staying in this lovely cottage on a magical
mountain side. I solved the Miss Gray mystery
too, but not sure that I can ever talk to her
about it, so I won't go into details now until I
get home. I can understand how she felt. It's
rather super really.
After so much travelling it's nice to be back in
Brittany again, but I'm feeling that there's
nothing else I really want to do here now. So
after a bit more time with Eleanor I'm planning
to come home in time for the August holidays.
We can have a good catch up then. Hope the
play went well. Do tell.
Love, Paula.

Paula seals the envelope, smiling to herself at all the
omissions in her letter. Several weeks earlier she would
have written much more fully. Now she feels no need
to share the detail. In fact she has deliberately blurred
the whole story. She has no intention of telling anyone
in New Zealand about Julien. They don't need to know.
They will certainly never learn from Eleanor. It's Paula's
private voyage. She prefers to save it for herself, to
savour the memories of the man she'll all too likely

never see again.

She sits at a table in one of the good back street restaurants in Concarneau, finishing her lunch and her letter, noticing the details that normally escape her in the company of other people. The immaculate blue table cloths are faded and crisp with laundering, the napkins to match. The silver is old and large, the china cheerfully bordered in blue. Below the aged stone walls are panels of blonde wood, not quite right with the huge adzed dark beams that criss-cross the ceiling. She has sipped her wine, enjoyed her escargots without minding being alone. Eleanor and Robert have gone to one of the cities, and she asked them to drop her in town for the day rather than stay alone at the house. She doesn't enjoy being alone in the country, she discovered when they were out another day. She knows she never will, that she needs people around her, whether she's acquainted with them or not. A solo lunch is pure self indulgence, a taste treat.

She thinks of her last visit to this restaurant, with Julien opposite her, both still rapt with awakened love. It was on their return from Ireland, an evening alone while Eleanor and Robert were visiting other friends. Yes, she was wildly in love with him. It seems strange that she's not any more. He's gone now, she doesn't need to know where. If it had only been the week in Ireland she might have stayed in love, been haunted by him, perhaps for ever. The extra time travelling has cured her, made her realise that what they share has no depth, no future. Their worlds are too far apart. It was enjoyable, but no longer significant. She was more interested in the places they visited, frustrated at his impatience when she wanted to spend extra time sight seeing, beyond his few hours of business. He was not so keen to walk the streets in the long evenings, to explore. He was only interested in eating, then bed, with her. She even forced him to several shows, a 'son et lumière' at an old cathedral. He did not enjoy it, scorning religious overtones, pouring his own

172

nationalistic scorn on the customs of both the Germans and the Spanish. She sensed the centuries of difference in his reactions, which she could not share.

It's a relief to be back in Brittany, returning to the peacefulness with Eleanor and Robert. She thinks Julien is relieved too. He doesn't stay long. She feels a little 'de trop' with the other couple, but they do nothing to make her feel that way. They all do as they please, no obligations except her own lack of independent transport. Even then she can walk to a nearby road to catch a bus. It doesn't take long to realise that she has achieved all she came for, and to start wondering about what is happening back at home. She's nearly ready to leave.

Her bread basket has gone. It was refilled after she emptied it soaking up the garlic butter from the snails. The friendly young woman removes her cheese plate, brings her tarte. She finishes her wine before eating it. She's calm, satisfied. Her escape has been completely detached from her real life. Now she will always have the private places of her mind into which to retreat, the memories she will never share.

A small black coffee completes her meal. Places are important. Ambience does affect the way you feel, the way things happen. She's sensitive to places. This one has just the right touches of style and warmth in the service, the excellence of the food. Her dish of 'raie' was superb, though she might never have considered eating stingray at home. In the future she will dream of French cuisine, want to return whenever possible.

She walks lazily along the coast later, stopping at the last beach to lie on the sand for a while, dreaming. Then just the time to walk back to the central café and her rendezvous with the others. She passes a travel shop, and deciding now is the time, goes in to alter her return flight, leaving herself just ten more days. She will be home in time to prepare for the children's holidays.

The others are already at the café. They immediately carry her off into the country to someone's small manor house by the river Odet, where they're all caught up in a dinner party, with Rémy and Anne-Marie joining them from Quimper.

It's not until the following afternoon, as the three of them laze in the orchard after lunch, that she has a chance to tell Eleanor her plans.

"You're going so soon?" Eleanor is startled. "I thought you'd be here longer than that."

"It's been so good, I've really appreciated the chance to come here. But I'm ready to leave now."

"You're not changing your plans because I'm here?" Robert is concerned.

"No, not at all. I just feel it's time to get home."

"For a first trip you have done a lot, certainly," Robert is pacified.

"I'll come back, I really will. Now I've found Nell again I shall want to return."

Eleanor and Robert exchange glances. Then he stands up suddenly, pausing for a moment behind Eleanor's chair, his hand on her shoulder. She reaches up and they hold hands briefly in silence, then he squeezes hers and turns away.

"I'm falling asleep in the sun. Think I'll have a proper siesta." He goes inside.

Eleanor picks a leaf out of her hair, staring after Robert. Paula is puzzled, moves her chair closer to her friend, feeling a sudden coolness as the sun hides behind a small fluffy cloud. She looks at Eleanor quizzically.

"I won't be here," Eleanor's words are simple, falling plainly, but somehow Paula is instinctively shocked by them.

"You're going away? For work? Will you come back to New Zealand?" There's silence for a while as the anxious questions hang in the still air. The sun comes out again. A bee lands in a sticky spill on the table and struggles to free itself.

"No Polly. No more work. No returning swallow to New Zealand. A few months, a year, and I won't be around at all." The words are still calm, as is the speaker.

Paula is stunned with shock. She stares at her friend, then flings herself at her to hold on to the reality of Eleanor, the solid flesh that her eyes are already too blinded to see.

"No! You can't die. I won't let you. There must be something we can do." Her horrified words echo shrilly in the quiet orchard.

"It's OK pal, really. I've known a while, made my choices." Eleanor partially extricates herself, looking lovingly at her friend.

"What do you mean?"

"It's cancer. Diagnosed some months ago. Too late to do anything."

"But surely there's something..."

"Oh I could have had chemotherapy, lost all my hair, my work, my health, everything that means anything to me. And it still may not have worked. I decided it wasn't for me. I'd go as I lived."

"But you're not sick, you look so good."

"So far. I'm on pills already, needing more and more."

"What will you do?"

"I assure you I won't hang around. There's a clinic in Switzerland. We'll go there when the time comes. Robert will help me end it before the worst."

"I can't believe it."

"You can't believe I'm going to die, or that I have decided to let myself without a fight?"

"Both. I'd be raging at the 'dying of the light'. Why aren't you?"

"Perhaps because I've already raged."

"How can you be so accepting?"

"It's not hard. Somebody has to make up those horrific statistics you keep seeing. It had to be someone you knew, some time."

Eleanor's voice is easy, calm. Paula is gathering her thoughts under the shock. It's too unreal, she can't imagine the world without Eleanor, she has become so alive to her, so important again over the summer. She sees her hand is shaking and tries to hide it. Eleanor takes it and holds it, her pulse strong. Her eyes hold Paula's gaze. She's too full of life to be dying. Paula blinks before speaking again.

"I couldn't be so philosophical. How can you bear to think about it?"

"Easy. There's nothing to keep me here, no real reason to hang around."

It still hasn't sunk in.

"Not even Robert?"

A slight shadow crosses Eleanor's face, then she smiles, a happy smile.

"He's stopping everything now to be with me to the end. Who could ask for more?"

"I'll stay. There must be something I can do for you."

"No Polly. There's nothing you can do. Don't distress yourself. We don't need anyone else."

"But..."

"No buts. Your family need you more. It's been great to see you. Thanks for coming like that."

"Now I understand."

"My urge to reclaim you from my past? Yes. When I thought about New Zealand there was nothing there that I wanted to go back to, or see again. Only you."

"I'll never forget that," Paula runs out of words, tears running down her cheeks.

"It really is all right. I don't intend to suffer." Eleanor slips from her chair to the grass, her arms going around her friend. Paula leans forward, holding the beloved head she has always admired so much, stroking the hair, the temples. Robert, looking from the upstairs window, sees them frozen as in a tableau, quickly sketching them on a pad to capture later in paint. He knows it's done. He comes downstairs to find the brandy and take it out to them.

Paula looks up to see Robert coming with the bottle, looking him full in the eyes for a long drawn out moment, in that instant envying her friend this man, this man who will share everything to the end in a complicity she can only dream about. She will return to her own fractured world. Perhaps Eleanor will even be better off in her calm certitude of what the future holds, such sublime control of destiny. She gulps her brandy too quickly and Eleanor, restored to her own seat, thumps her back, laughing.

"Pour her another, Robert. This has turned into a wake, and I like laughter at wakes. It should be a celebration."

In an odd way, it is. They make the evening a special occasion too. There is fresh seafood from the market, veal, a raspberry tarte. Paula helps Robert prepare it while Eleanor sets the table under the trees with the checked cloth, a row of glasses, and some special wines Robert has been saving. They laugh over the meal, the late sun shining through the old trees, their langoustine shells tossed into a bowl on the grass. When Paula rises to help with the next course her chair tips and she stumbles over the leg of it, sprawling on the ground. Eleanor laughs so much she joins her, slipping off her chair and leaving Robert to bring out the carefully chosen cheeses, pouring more burgundy to go with them.

Paula raises her glass with the others, holding on to the moment, not letting her mind recognise that time is running out in too many ways for her comprehension. When the laughter is thinning and the tarte is finished, Robert makes coffee and they sit in silence, watching the fingers of colour from the setting sun fade through the motionless evening branches. They share the peacefulness, close and comfortable, no more words needed.

Paula moves carefully in the morning, nursing a fragile head. They stay at home for the day, not making any effort to leave their chairs in the orchard. Robert laughs at them, serving light meals then disappearing into his work. In the evening they walk to the coast and along it, planning to catch the market the next day. It may be Paula's last market before it is time to take the route to Paris and her plane connection.

Paula thinks there cannot be any more surprises. Nora's letter proves her wrong.

Dear Paula,
Your succession of postcards from different places has been a delight. I had to get my atlas out to follow your travels. You should be back in Brittany by now and I suspect it is up to me to break some sad news to you.
Your friend Virginia Gray has passed away, quite suddenly. I had actually been spending quite a bit of time with her. In all the time I have known her she has always been so self sufficient. Just recently she seemed to want company more, although of course she never asked, it was entirely my own feeling. She was always keen for news of you, and I think missed you very much. You are good company my dear. I would call in every time I was in town and have a coffee with her. Sometimes I managed to get her to come out with me to the coffee bar when she was not busy and the girl could cope. We had to leave the phone number in case. The Women's Guild we both belong to had a dinner and we went to it together. She seemed to enjoy it very much. It was only a day or two later that she collapsed in the shop. She was barely conscious in hospital by the time the girl rang to let me know. She couldn't think who else to call. I had a little while with Virginia before she slipped into unconsciousness. She asked to be remembered warmly to you, and I assured her she was in your thoughts. I also promised to look after the shop, which I have been doing. She died that night. A brain haemorrhage they said. At least it was quick.

However that is not the only news. When her will was revealed, you were a beneficiary. You share the inheritance of her home and business with an unknown woman in Ireland, Siobhan Grogan. The lawyer has written to the address and I enclose it for you in case you would like to get in touch while you're in that part of the world. If of course she can be found. The lawyer seemed doubtful that there had been any contact between them for many years. It seems she had no relations, unless the girl is one. I will not enlarge on the local speculation about her when the news spread somehow.

So be philosophical my dear. I'm sure you could not have done more than you did for her, and that you gave her a lot of pleasure in all the time you shared. She was not an easy person to know, and you must have been closer to her than most of us.

Don't be alarmed, I am not over extending myself at the shop. Young Susan is really very capable, and I have already found an older woman who is proving invaluable and could probably take over if that is what you want on your return. Gordon has been very good helping when he can, especially with the accounts, and calling in to take me out to lunch.

Roz comes in too, and we had a Wednesday lunch the other day and talked about you. You mustn't worry. No need to come rushing back, the lawyer said there is no urgency to deal with everything. It's old Mr Copeland and you know that urgency is not one of his trademarks.

So there we are my dear. Time moves on for us all. Virginia left a letter for you that will of course be waiting for you to open. The lawyer apparently held it with her will.

Gordon asked me to send his love. He is very busy and suspects he mightn't have written last

*week. These men. How can they 'suspect' they
haven't written. I 'suspect' he is not very well
organised without you, but it is good for him
and you must not give up any newfound wings
of independence just to 'organise' for Gordon.
Do continue to make the most of your time
away. We'll still be here when you return so
don't hurry. Enjoy your friend. She sounds a
remarkable woman and I would very much like
to meet her one day.
With fondest love,
Nora.*

Paula sits blinking over coffee as she reads. It's the
café near the Post Office. Some instinct lead her to go
there to read her mail rather than the usual meeting
place with the others. It's not until she reaches the part
where Nora talks about how much she would like to
meet Eleanor, that the reality of the rest of the letter hits
her, linked to that. Nora will never meet Eleanor.
Somehow that is more immediate and shattering than
anything else. They would have got on well together.
Miss Gray's death seems remote and unreal, it hasn't
yet reached her feelings, she's numb. As for the rest,
she can't begin to take it in. Nora running the shop?
For her? It's too much of a shock on top of everything
else.

She's so late that Eleanor comes looking for her at the
Post Office. She notices her pass the door, then come
back, seeing her and coming to join her.

"What's happened?" she knows immediately. "You're
in shock. Tell me." Eleanor orders a brandy and takes
her hand. Paula manages a laugh, shaky, but still a
laugh. Here's Eleanor, very much alive. Everything must
be all right.

"It's OK. It's not the family. Miss Gray's died
suddenly."

"Oh, dear Polly, what an awful shock for you. You
weren't expecting that. I'm so sorry," Eleanor puts her

180

arm around Paula's shoulders. Paula looks up and sees her friend's eyes are already brimming in sympathy. They hug each other in silence, then Eleanor hands Paula her own brandy to replace the one she has just drunk without noticing. Her coffee arrives as well.

"Nora has written to tell me. It seems she's left me the shop, or half of it."

"Well! That's a surprise."

"Totally. The other beneficiary is William's daughter."

"And she'll never know you met. Isn't that strange."

"Rather wonderful really," Paula revives. Trust Eleanor to do the right thing.

"Well you must phone her. Phone him. Phone Nora."

Paula laughs as Eleanor's enthusiasm takes over.

"He'll be sad," she remembers those eyes, her thoughts of the connection between them and Miss Gray's.

"It sounds as if he'd not forgotten anything."

"Oh no. That was obvious. He still thought about her."

"Do you think you should go back?"

"That's a thought. Siobhan should have heard from the lawyer by now. I'll phone and see."

"You didn't think the daughter knew about Miss Gray."

"No. I may be wrong."

"Come on. You need a meal. Robert's waiting with the shopping."

They take food home and eat at leisure in the orchard again. Paula thinks how much she'll miss it all, how summer in the orchard with Eleanor will stay etched in her mind forever. Eternal. A kind of peak of existence, a blueprint of reality, however remote it might be from what she thought her whole life before.

Already her life is falling into two parts, before her journey, her time with Eleanor, and after, when nothing will ever be quite the same. Miss Gray and the shop are part of that, part of the inevitability of this movement of life, and death, that sweeps her along. She seems to be able to see things more clearly and intently than ever before, an intensified vision. She tries to describe it to Eleanor as they doze after lunch, Robert breathing heavily and fast asleep in the shade.

"You always used to analyse things too much," Eleanor is comfortably light.

"Did I? Maybe that was the last time I ever did really think about my life."

"Nothing like a bit of eschatology to get you to reassess how you see things."

"Long time since I've heard that word."

"It's a good word. People don't want to think about death though. Not till they're forced to."

Paula looks at her friend, lying back in the outside seat under the trees. How can she bear to leave, knowing she will never see her again? Then she chides herself, realising how fortunate she is to have seen Eleanor again at all, how she will treasure every moment of this holiday in the future. She mustn't let herself become too sentimental when Eleanor is so calm.

"I suppose you've thought about death a lot."

"It was a shock to start with. But Robert has been my saviour. Nothing like sharing a death to cement a relationship."

"How can you be so flippant?"

"You have to laugh. What's the alternative?"

"One of the things I've always remembered about you is your capacity for fun and laughter."

"Life is pretty bizarre. There's always something to laugh about."

"I admired you for it. More than ever now."

"Don't put me on a pedestal Polly. It's only because I couldn't cope with pain and suffering that I'm making these choices. Remember how I used to fear needles?"

"Yes. You fainted when we had the tuberculosis shots."

"Now I can cope with needles, but any other treatment is beyond me. Just going to hospital is too much for me."

"Clinics in the mountains always sound rather

romantic. Katherine Mansfield territory, the Fitzgeralds."

"Yes. We've chosen a lovely spot, be sure of that. No need to spare expense now."

"Oh Nell."

"Stop it Polly. I won't have you maudlin. Reassess your own life by all means, but don't mourn me."

"You've helped me see what's really important. I won't waste so much time in future."

"Don't get pious either. It's not you."

"I think studying in Auckland will be a good idea."

"All power to you. If you'd just gone back to that small town and done nothing I would have haunted you, I promise."

"But my bookshop?"

"That's a retirement position. Save it till then, if you want to."

"I wonder if Siobhan would like it." Paula thinks of the capable young woman in Ireland. She can see her running a business. It's not so easy to see her in Rivertown.

"Interesting concept. I suppose Ireland's not too different if they moved."

"She might prefer to stay nearer her father."

"I expect your Miss Gray's letter will suggest you offer to buy her out, send them the money."

"I hadn't thought of that. Clever you."

"On the other hand, new Irish life in Rivertown could stir it up a bit." Eleanor grins at her. Paula visualises Rivertown, the impact on the main street of the large bearded Irishman and his family.

"Could be rather fun. Wouldn't the town talk if the Grogans arrived in Miss Gray's place!"

"But you'll be spending part of the year in Auckland anyway."

"That won't be for long."

Going to Auckland has become fact. Paula can see that Eleanor approves. She puts out of her mind the long list of probable obstacles to achieving her dream.

She thinks Nora will be an ally. She's confident it will happen.

"William would be a great chap to have around." Paula speculates.

"Probably a bit old for you. And that would certainly send the whole place up in smoke!"

"If he kept the memory of his Virginie intact all this time it would take more than me to shake it."

"You'd better go gently on breaking the news, if the lawyer's letter hasn't arrived."

"What news? Lawyers?" Robert wakes suddenly, startled. They fill him in, then Eleanor goes to make fresh coffee, leaving them to talk. Paula feels so comfortable with this gentle man, happy to know that Eleanor has such a close friend to be with her.

"I think you would enjoy a book shop of your own. Don't you?" Robert is thoughtful.

"Yes I would. I've had several ideas before about expanding the business. Maybe having a second hand section as well. I'm sure the town could do with that."

"There you are then. Don't let Eleanor push you into becoming a city person if you are not. Try it all out, then see what you want."

"I will. Thanks Robert. I'm so glad you're here for Eleanor."

"I'm glad too. She means everything to me." Paula knows that is the truth. "Don't you worry too much about her."

"Not with you here. You'll let me know?"

"Of course. We'll stay in touch."

Eleanor returns with the tray.

Paula looks at her two friends, counting the days she has left with them. Even while the time seems poised in expectation it still speeds on. The idle sunny afternoons, flung motionless in the orchard, are slipping away far too quickly. Going beyond return, even as it is all preserved in her mind forever, a tranquil picture of happiness, untouchable.

Chapter Eighteen

It's nearly a year later that the large awkward parcel arrives. Paula has driven back home for midterm break in what used to be Miss Gray's Morris Minor, now hers, chugging along as sedately as ever, to her enormous pleasure. She's high on her studies after the first half year, looking forward to continuing research, perhaps eventual writing. She's kept the shop, sold Miss Gray's house, and writes regularly to Siobhan, who bought her own shop in Ireland with her share of the money, making a small living for herself and her child. A friend of Nora's manages the bookshop back home. Paula knows now that she'll continue to enjoy working there, expanding it later. The small town is more satisfying for her than the city.

She looks at the wrappings of the parcel. It comes from Switzerland. Her last letters from Eleanor have been enthusiastic about the move to Switzerland, all the exploring she is doing with Robert. She never discusses her own health, keeping the same cheerful chatty tone of the Eleanor Polly cherishes. She turns the parcel over and sees the lawyer's stamp on the back. Her heart flips. Her hands shake as she tears off the wrappings, revealing the large oblong cardboard framework. It falls open to the huge painting, the colour thick on the canvas. It is herself and Eleanor in the orchard. She can almost hear the bees, the cicadas, the birds. Robert has captured the moment forever. Each detail of leaf, of flower, of clothing, as she sits in the chair, Eleanor on the grass at her feet, leaning on her knees. Their faces are calm, solemn but hopeful, looking at each other with one of those eternal looks of friendship and understanding. Complicity.

She props it against a chair, feasting on it. The envelope falls to the floor as she does so. A mist of tears makes the letter hard to read. It takes time to comprehend that Eleanor is dead, that Robert is following her last instructions in sending Paula the painting. His letter is brief and gentle, saying he will write more fully later. He encloses a letter from Eleanor. Another parcel will follow for her, but he wanted to send the painting immediately.

Eleanor has written her a poem. In the old lighthearted doggerel, designed to make her laugh. It does. Laugh and cry and hug to herself a special part of her life. Then she smiles. She knows now that in her mind's eye she will always see a smile in response. From Eleanor.